The Vice President

The Rise Of The Word-Command Killer

The Independent Adjudicator

Written By
Elina Salajeva

Created By
Elinadeivid

DISCLAIMER

This is a work of fiction. Names, characters, businesses, places, events, and incidents are either the products of the author's imagination or used in a fictitious manner. Any resemblance to actual persons, living or dead, or actual events is purely coincidental.

DEDICATION

To Accountability and Rebuilding the World.

Touchladybirdlucky Studios
A David Gomadza Production.
Elina Salajeva, Elinadeivid have asserted their rights
under Copyright, Designs and Patents Act 1988 to be
identified as the author of this work.
ISBN: 978-1-9164397-3-3
[Touchladybirdlucky Studios]
ISBN: 978-1546630418
[Createspace]
Copyright © 2017 Elina Salajeva, Elinadeivid.
All rights reserved.

ACKNOWLEDGMENTS

Many thanks and best wishes to the Elinadeivid brand. Big thanks also to Touchladybirdlucky Studios.

CHAPTER ONE

Dorothy started walking slowly as if warming up her legs. Slowly and gradually she increased the speed, ending up running a little faster. She proceeded to increase her speed until her pace was sprint. Her heart beat increased as the constant pounding from her feet drove the motor giving it enough horsepower to see the belt rotate faster and faster as she sprints. She was wearing the Elinadeivid trainers. Droplets of sweat covered the treadmill conveyor belt that seemed to be dancing to the pull effect of the motor inside the treadmill. The conveyor belt looked shiny as the Elinadeivid trainers seemed to have been polishing it with every step. The heat from the spinning motor gave the false shining effect as well, otherwise the grip between the Elinadeivid trainers and the treadmill conveyor belt was undoubtedly strong that Dorothy seemed unconcerned about a slip or a fall. The Elinadeivid trainers seemed to be doing some magic but in fact it was the skill of the lady. The way she handled the cycles said it all. She had been doing this for some time now. The soft silk fabric shorts she was wearing were so tightly fitting that her true shape could be easily seen, very athletic built. Her naval was exposed, and she was wearing a small vest that covered half her body cupping her breasts tightly. Sweat was running down her face, some down her neck and her body and into the groove between her breasts. She was wearing a small necklace that swung back and forth with every step she made. In front of her was a big screen. A projected video of a woman was playing showing her running in the park surrounded by beautiful trees and vegetation. Dorothy imitated every move she made. It seemed she had been running for quiet sometime now. The video it seemed was driving her as she seemed very energetic and determined to carry on matching every step the woman in the video made. A beautiful blond lady entered the gym wearing a baseball cap and sun glasses. Her name, Liana. She was caring a gym bag. She walked straight to the huge mirror on the wall. After putting her bag on the bench, she posed in front of the mirror. She looked at herself and smiled. She turned aside and looked at her back-view. She pressed down her bum. She faced the mirror and pulled her vest up and lowered the front part of her shorts to reveal her full stomach and the forming six-packs. She looked in the mirror before she started warming up. She stretched her legs. Minutes later she was on the cycling machine pushing the pedals very hard and very fast swerving left and right. Sweat was disappearing down her tight-fitting top. She had earphones, and she looked focused looking at the huge mirror in front of her. Later the gym was packed with a lot of trainers. Dorothy walked toward the door before looking around. She spotted Liana and looked at her as she powered through the cycling. She stood there and observed Liana for some time. Liana noticed that she was watching her. Liana smiled and raised her hand and gave a gesture asking Dorothy to come over. Dorothy looked at her watch. She pointed at the watch before gesturing with her hand as if talking on the phone. She soon disappeared. Liana finished cycling and took her stuff and walked toward the shower rooms. As she entered the shower room, she heard Dorothy singing. After taking a quick shower Dorothy came out of the shower cubicle using the big towel she squeezed the water from her hair. Liana came out as well with a cloth round her body. She looked at Dorothy who was butt naked.

"Looking fabulous Dorothy."

"Thanks. I am trying. I must be at my best you know. How is it going with you?"

"Pretty good been training hard as well."

"Have you made up your mind yet?"

"I think I have to pass. There are so many things that have not been fully explained you know. I must find out first. What about you?"

"Liana, nothing to lose for me. I am in. A free vacation and a chance to earn loads of money."

"Are you not afraid of the risks? What if something goes wrong?"

"What can go wrong? If it does. Still it's worth what's on offer. I just must know my game. A few more weeks training and I am done. Ready like never. That's life you know."

"I guess you are right. I have to put my head around it."

The two ladies spoke for a while before leaving the gym.

Liana entered her convertible black Mercedes Benz and dialed someone.

"Have you got anything for me yet?"

"We can't talk over the phone. Can we meet my place say seven o'clock at night tomorrow?"

"OK, see you."

At the airport, a lot of people are going their way. A loud voice from the airport PA system was heard announcing the arrivals and departures of planes to different gates. In the lobby were a lot of people sitting with expectantly happy faces. Everyone, it seemed was anxiously and excitedly waiting for the arrival of their loved ones. Everyone waited impatiently. A young lady looked at the big screen above and smiled. She walked toward the arrivals gate and enthusiastically with a bright face stood in anticipation. Minutes later the green light at the arrivals gate doors, illuminated to a bright florescent green color. Everyone else stood up and walked toward the gate. People started coming out of the gates and instantaneously as they came out they would hug with their friends and relatives. That went on for some time. Later the gate lights turned to red and the automatic doors closed. A woman stood in front of the gates and looked around surprised and confused as well. She looked around and found out that all the people who had originally gathered there had gone. It was now only her and another man who were still sat in the arrival lobby. She looked around and tried to dial a number on her phone. She paced left and right before she walked toward the automatic doors. She pressed a button on the doors and someone answered on the intercom system.

"How can I help you?"

"Are there passengers from flight 7 still to check out? It seemed the gates have been closed and my husband did not come out."

"Everyone from flight 7 has alighted and checked out. Is your husband part of the crew madam?"

"What? No, he was a passenger."

"Are you sure he boarded this plane?"

"Very sure I spoke to him just before he boarded this plane. Can you check if he was in the plane and what happened to him?"

"I am afraid that information is confidential I can't tell you who was in or not in the plane."

"So, how do I know where my husband is? I am sure he boarded this plane?"

"Check with the reception desk they will give you a phone number for the airline concerned and dial them direct."

The person on the other end paused for a while before carrying on.

"Unless."

There was a moment of silence. The woman asking for her husband, her name was Abigail. As soon as she had heard this her heart felt like she had been pierced with a sword. She froze for a while not knowing what to say. Strange frightening thoughts clouded her brain. It was until after she accepted the possibility of her husband being thrown out of the plane that she calmed down.

"Unless what?" She asked frantically searching for clues.

"Are you sure he was alive?"

Abigail did not answer straight away. She felt a lump choking her throat. She tried clearing her throat first.
"Hello! Are you still there?"
A moment passed before Abigail replied.
"What do you mean? What are you implying? What makes you even suggest such an unthinkable idea?"
"Just bear with me for a while. Please hold the line."
The line was still connected, but the responder had gone away. Voices could be heard in the background. Abigail looked around her and looked at the man still sitting in the lobby. The man looked unconcerned or unmoved. She remembered the time she first arrived at the airport. She recalled seeing the man sat there. It had been more than an hour now and the man was still in the same place. He looked like he had been drinking. Abigail remembered seeing the man shoving what appeared to be a whiskey bottle in his jacket. She recalled the first time she met Divante. He was such a charmer. She knew straight away that he was the man of her dreams. Their life was a bliss until his headquarters moved abroad. That's when everything started. He changed within a few weeks. He started drinking. Although she knew he loved drinking she also knew that he was much into wine other than anything else. Even herself growing up she had witnessed her dad have a glass of wine after every meal. This was nothing to be alarmed at, but recently her husband had been drinking spirits. As she was busy pondering about this, a door on the other side of the reception desk labeled private only no admittance suddenly opened. A woman dressed in uniform appeared and walked toward her. A man appeared from the other door and stopped in front of Abigail.

"Hello, madam. We have a coffin on the plane of a male."

Abigail looked shocked, confused, and saddened. She did not say anything but looked at the other female in uniform walking toward her.

"No! No!" Shouted Abigail clutching her head.

The lady in the uniform approached her. She noticed fear written on Abigail's face and tried to calm her down.

"Very sorry madam can you follow me. Body is ready for collection."

Abigail staggered toward the door following the woman in uniform. Somehow instinctively she stopped and looked in the waiting lobby. The man who was seated in the lobby as soon as he had seen the woman in uniform got up and walked toward her following Abigail and the woman. Abigail looked at him.

The woman in uniform stopped and looked backward.

"Something wrong, madam?"

"I don't think we are talking about the same person. I am looking for my husband. He is not dead."

The woman in uniform looked at the clip board in her hand.

"Mr. Wrexman Johns?"

The old man raised his hand and urged forward. Abigail smiled, confused but relieved that it was not her husband. The lady in uniform sensed Abigail's joy that at least there was hope that it was not her husband.

"Not my husband!" Shouted Abigail.

"But where is he?" She asked herself not expecting any answer from the lady in the uniform.

"Check with the airline first."

The lady and the old man entered through the doors next to the reception leaving Abigail standing for a while. Later she was talking with the airline operator.

"I am sure my husband boarded the plane. We spoke just before the plane took off."

"As far as we know everyone alighted the plane. There was a body on the plane and you said that was not your husband. I will need my managers permission before I can give you passenger information over the phone."

"How long can that take?"

"I will do my best please stay on the line."

So many questions were running in Abigail's mind. What had happened to her husband? Why he did not call or even said something. Were the rumors true that he was seeing someone else abroad? Abigail looked more confused than ever before.

"Hello, are you still there?" Shouted the operator.

"I can confirm that your husband alighted this flight but."

The operator did not finish talking. There was a moment of silence.

"But what? Where is he then?"

"I am afraid there was an incident. He passed away on board the flight."

"What!? How? Are you sure? Where is he?"

"Stay in the lobby someone will be with you?"

Abigail felt distraught, she felt her world collapsing before her eyes. She felt like she wanted to die too. Divante was her life. How could something like this happen to her? What on earth had she done wrong to deserve to be robbed of the love of her life? She sat in the reception lobby for a few minutes but it seemed like a long time to her. Sank in the lobby sofas it seemed she was disoriented and confused by all this. Tears of pain rolled down her cheeks as she sobbed like a baby. She could not even phone anyone. She wanted to see his body first. It was like a dream. She couldn't believe this was happening. She begged God that this turns out to be some mistake. She promised to do whatever it takes to never leave her husband. Fear crippled her as the door on the side of the reception opened and two people came out of the door. A woman dressed in uniform and a man dressed in an expensive suit. Her heart beat fast with every step they made toward her. She could hear the noise made by their footsteps thumbing in her ear drums as they approached. It was frightening. In a small voice, she was chanting and praying to wake up from this nightmare.

"We are very sorry madam for your loss can you please follow us we will talk in private."

Abigail looked lost as she remained sat there. It seemed she was in a world of her own. The man had to repeat what he had originally said before Abagail stood up and staggered toward the door next to the reception. The room looked small. It had so many things inside that the impression was that there was not enough space left. In general, this was a normal room. There was a huge table with a PA system. There was computer equipment everywhere as well. There was a big couch, a desk and few chairs around it. There was a big cabinet-like box with electrical cables coming out of it. The man opened the door and pointed his hand inside. Abigail walked in followed by the female in uniform.

"My name is Jo Ranks call me JR, and this is Anita the airport customer assistant. I am with the national security division. I would like to ask you a few questions regarding your husband."

"Where is his body? I want to see my husband now. National security? What does that have to do with my husband?"

JR looked at Anita first before answering.

"I am afraid you cannot see the body of your husband. This case is now a matter of national security. You will be able to see your husband after we are satisfied that it is right for you to do so."

"Bullshit. That's my husband we are talking about here. National security what? He is not a terrorist so what gives you the right to deny me access to his body." Queried Abigail standing up and pacing left and right the small office.

"I want to see my husband now. Take me to his body."

There was a moment of silence. JR looked down for a while before looking at Anita.

"This is for your own safety."

"What do you mean? He is my husband. How can he be a threat to national security? I thought you said he is dead?"

"It's not him. I think or should I say. The consensus right now is that he is a Trojan horse. We have reasons to believe that the way he died he must have been murdered."

"But you said that he died in the plane, murdered by who?" Asked Abigail shocked and confused.

"Probably this is not the best time to talk about this. We will need your contact details and get back to you after you have grieved for your loss."

"Who decides the right time? I want to see my husband now. I am not leaving without seeing him. What are you covering up? Did you murder my husband? As far as I know he was alive just before takeoff. If you have murdered my husband, I will make sure that you will pay for this. I want to see my husband now."

JR stood up and dialed a number. He raised his index finger before going out of the office.

Abigail sat down and as she looked at Anita, emotionally overwhelmed she broke down and cried. Anita stood up and walked to the couch and sat next to Abigail, hesitantly she put her arms around her. Abigail laid her head on her shoulder and cried uncontrollably.

JR returned to find the women in each other's arms both sobbing. Quickly Anita stood up and wiped her eyes holding back her tears. JR threw a staring glance at her as if saying that that was very unprofessional.

JR looked at Abigail and leaned forward.

"My boss has agreed to let you see the footage the time he died. After our investigations, we will show you the body. The truth is that the body is not here now. It has been moved to a safe place."

"You are not listening to me. I said I want to see the body of my husband not some footage. If he is already dead why worry about his safety?"

"We are following protocol madam. I am afraid you have to wait the body has been flown to a secured place away from the major activities in the city."

"You sound like he has some disease. Show me the footage."

"It's not a disease, madam. He might be a bomb."

JR and Anita exchanged a quick glance. Abigail sat back in her couch.

"Bomb! My husband? Are you out of your mind?"

"Can we watch the footage first please?" Pleaded JR.

JR stood up and inserted a small chip into the machine in front of him. Soon afterward footage appeared of Divante walking toward the lobby. He looked anxious as he kept looking around him and especially behind him. He quickly urged forward the queue. Moments later two men arrived wearing expensive suits. Somehow Divante seemed to have ducked. The footage seemed to change focus as Divante was later shown in the queue about to board a plane. He still looked anxious and worried it seemed. A lady in stilettos appeared from nowhere and started walking toward him. The airport attended seemed to stop her, but she resisted and urged forward to Divante. She seemed as if stopping him to go. The footage showed them as struggling for a while before the woman slapped him and walked away. Even at this point Divante seemed worried as he kept looking around him. The screen went blank and Abigail stood up.

"Even if he was cheating on me that can't explain his death. What are you hiding?"

"Madam Abigail please let's watch the footage first." Insisted JR

Soon after the next footage shows Divante suddenly falling to the ground. He was in the tunnel about to board the plane. People around him moved away from him as he struggled. Somehow it looked like he was being beaten up, but to everyone's surprise there was no one around him that close to be doing the damage. He stood up and soon fell to the ground as if he had received a heavy blow to the head. The bleeding from the nose, mouth and ears said it all. He was being attacked by the ghosts. Everyone looked at each other shocked and scared. Most run away after witnessing that. He seemed to be calling for help. He even tried to talk into the camera in the corner. Soon after he laid on the floor. Blood was bleeding from everywhere, his head, face noise mouth and ears. It was gruesome to watch. A lot of blood drenched the tunnel carpet that it could only be explained by heavy internal bleeding. The time the airline security arrived he had died, his eyes wide open.

"So, madam Abigail. No matter how gruesome this is and I must say shocking as it is. The airport security is not responsible for your husband 's death. You have seen the footage yourself. I must admit the only thing I have witnessed close to that was when a man was hit by a lorry. He bled out all his blood within seconds. Now you can see for yourself why we think this is a matter of national security. Abigail looked really frightened. Her face had become very pale like she had seen a ghost.

"Does the woman we saw earlier on have something to do with this? She might have set him up. She looked very upset."

"Could be or could not be. One thing is for sure whatever it is it is greater and more dangerous than what we have seen. Now you understand why we think it's a matter of national security? The way he died is unprecedented."

"He looked worried, it seemed he was running away. Did you see how he kept looking around him. I think he was afraid of someone else." Added Anita

"Was this the date he originally planned to come back? From the video, it seemed he was running away of some kind. I checked with the airline he purchased the ticket last minute it seemed someone else had canceled at the last minute."

"It was a surprise to me. Yesterday he phoned me and said that he had missed me and wanted to come home but I was not expecting him for another two weeks." Replied Abigail.

"Whoever is behind this did not want him to leave. In fact, I think they only knew last minute that he was leaving. That could explain why they murdered him just before he boarded the plane."

"Why before boarding the plane if they wanted him dead they could have killed him in the plane or when he was here?"

"The initial thinking is that he has something they did not want him to leave with. Killing him in the tunnel would make the airplane refuse carrying him aboard as they had to complete paperwork and inform the authorities first before carrying his body."

"So how did he end up on board, dead and without the necessary paperwork?"

"After my initial investigation. I have found out that the pilot was behind schedule already. Any deal would not only complicate things but jeopardize the flight too. So, I guess that could be the idea behind his reasoning."

"I understand he was not on the original flight manifest as the seat he bought was a last-minute cancelation making it easy for the pilot to get away with it if you know what I mean."

Abigail sat down scared and confused.

"So, who killed my husband and why?"

In one of the suburbs a motorbike passed the main road raving loud as it sped past one of the houses. A cat sneaked inside the house through the opening in the door after hearing the motorbike noise. It made its way upstairs and straight into one of the bedrooms. The bedroom was spacious with huge mirrors on the roof. There was a small dressing table near the bed. On the dressing table was a medium flat screen. The cat jumped onto the bed and walked toward a woman who was sleeping. The woman woke up and grabbed the cat. She kissed the cat raising it in the air with its body hanging downward. The cat mews. The lady placed the cat down and flicked a remote control. Soon after an automated voice was played from the flat screen.

"Good morning Miss. Liana. You have two appointments today. First with the jewelry dealer at 10 am and then with the tattooist in the afternoon. Have a wonderful day."

Shortly after Liana picked up the phone and dialed a number.

"Yes, it's me. I am ready."

"That's great. Come to the office. I have already arranged your appointments for today."

"Why I need to go to the jewelry dealer? I am not into tattoos either you know." Said Liana.

"That's all part of the deal. You must look modern go with the current trend. I will explain when we meet. If that's all goodbye."

CHAPTER TWO

Darrell woke up to the beeping sound of his watch. He got up and switched on his laptop. He quickly went through his security program. After a while he cursed. A message was flashing on the screen. He quickly typed something on the keyboard. He tried to synchronize his watch and the laptop. Frantically he collected what he needed and rushed out of the house. He looked around and got into his car. Soon he drove out of the yard and headed to the city. He looked very nervous. A beeping sound pierced the air, and he looked sideways panicking resulting in him swerving the car in the road in the process. He quickly looked at his watch. A flashing message was displayed on the screen. After driving for a while constantly looking in the rear-view mirror and side mirrors he noticed a car following behind. Instincts kicked in and he felt nervous and stepped on the gas. After checking again in the rear mirror, he realized that he was right. He had company, someone was after him. He knew this could mean death. He had heard about this but never seemed to believe it until now. This was an escape or die situation. Someone was after him. Someone powerful enough to have wiped off his bank account balances and all his connections overnight. He remembered going for the defensive driving course months before. This was no coincidence. He knew at one time he would need the skills he had lent even after years of driving. Darrel was a man who always followed his instincts. That could explain in part why he was one of the most successful entrepreneurs. Rumors he had heard and strange happenings for the past weeks had given him sleepless nights. Since the day someone broke into his house, Darrel had been stressed up and unable to relax. He was at the top of his life, enjoying success when terrible things started happening. Lately he had been suspicious and unable to focus and concentrate of his business empire. While pondering the events of the past weeks a car slammed into his causing his car to swerve off the road briefly before he gained control again. As soon as he was back in the road, he noticed that there were two cars chasing him one being a black land rover. He looked in the rear-view mirror and when he looked back in the road, he was partly driving on the other lane used by oncoming vehicles. If he had not reacted swiftly like he did, he could have had a head-on collision with a lorry. The sound of the horns from the lorry nearly deafened him putting him into extra alert mood. He instantly swerved the car causing him to go off the road nearly crashing into a parked car nearby. He quickly found his way back into the road. When he looked in the rear-view mirror, he noticed three cars behind following at cruising speeds. For the first time in his life fear crippled him. He had never felt so afraid. This was it. He had one choice escape or die. These people meant business. They had destroyed all his financial assets and wiped out all his connections overnight. He anticipated a huge problem in the road ahead. He was now approaching a residential area with parked cars nearby. He looked in the side mirrors and remembered the driving training he had taken a few weeks back. This somehow restored his confidence. For the first-time bullets were fired at him damaging the side mirrors. The screeching of car wheels sends everyone panicking and running out of the way. Darrell drove his car using both lanes and swerving side to side. A car towing a caravan was coming from ahead and the space for him to pass was narrow. At the current speed, he was driving there were likely to be problems ahead. Determined and fearing for his life he held the steering wheel very tight. As he approached the car, the driver of the car towing the car panicked and swerved out of the road but this swerved the caravan in front of Darrell's car. He was cornered, no choice and space to maneuver to as on the side road there were parked cars. His car broke the side mirrors of the parked cars and as soon as he passed the car he held the steering wheel firmly. His car hit the end part of the caravan sending it crashing onto the parked cars and damaging it in the process. His car was damaged on the side as well but he continued driving. He looked in the rear-view mirror hoping the cars following him will stop as well. To his dismay the cars made it through too. Ahead was a bend in the road. He reduced the speed and turned only to find a narrower road ahead and a car waiting in the middle of the road giving way to oncoming vehicles. He instantly pressed the brakes and reversed as fast as he can. The other cars chasing him were approaching. The screeching of car wheels caused everyone nearby to panic. He reversed into the front vehicle chasing him. He quickly drove through a gap between parked cars onto the pedestrian pavement. He blasted the horn frequently and people jumped sideways getting out of his way. One of the cars followed his car onto the pavement but the other cars remained in the main road. He looked in the rear-view mirror and saw the car still chasing him. He looked side ways to his left and saw the two other cars in the road nearly parallel to his car. Shots were fired sending him ducking and as soon as he looked ahead on the pavement he was kids in the road. He blasted the horn continuously and when he looked ahead, he saw an opening in the parked cars and accelerated harshly. Shortly afterward he was back in the road nearly crashing into another oncoming car. The oncoming car swerved hitting the parked car. The car behind rammed into the back of his car causing his car to jerk forward. Momentarily after the back windscreen of his car was smashed with bullets. As he lifted his head, he saw a lorry ahead of him. He tried to overtake the lorry but there was an oncoming traffic and quickly he swerved back to his lane. He tried again and as soon as he was about to pass the lorry. He felt a stinging feeling in his neck and a feeling of warm water running down his neck. Soon after a large bang was heard and the car burst into flames. The following cars screeched their tires to a halt. Four men jumped out of their cars and opened fire. A well dressed up man got out of the limousine holding the day's newspaper. He was wearing a big coat and a suit inside. The way he walked pointed to some sort of urgency. A man who seemed to be his secretary got out of the limo and followed him pacing very fast after him. The man in front was called Sean mid-fifties with a balding head and glasses. He looked very upset about something. After punching a code, he entered the huge city building. Jimmy his secretary was following behind trying to catch up with him. Sean entered the lift and did not have the courtesy to hold the lift doors for Jimmy. As Jimmy arrived in the corridor breathing heavily he only saw a glimpse of Sean as the lift doors were nearly closing. He rushed and tried to stop the doors from closing. Something big was on the cards. Since getting the job some years ago this is the first time he had seen Sean reacting like this. Jimmy waited for the next lift on the other side. The lift doors opened and Jimmy entered the lift. As soon as the lift doors opened on the level he was after, he saw Sean entering his office followed by three well-dressed men. The door soon closed behind him and he heard Sean locking the door behind him. Sean was fuming with anger. The wrinkly lines on his face sold him out. As soon as the three men saw his face, they knew something was up. This was not the Sean they are used to, no. He had changed overnight. As he sat down in his chair Sean's belly seemed too big to let him sit comfortably. He had walked very fast entering the building. He was now breathing heavily and droplets of sweat could be seen forming on his forehead. He corrected his tie and loosened his cross-belts.

"Gentlemen I had a call yesterday from the Vice President. It was brought to my attention that you had not followed protocol and risked the lives of passengers on board. With regret, I would like to inform you all that you have been dismissed with immediate effect without any appeal or pay."

Bankz, one of the pilot, a man in his late forties with thousands of flying hours to his name got up and walked toward the window. He pushed his hair backward and sighed for a while. He walked back to his chair and sat down. He leaned forward and looked at Sean straight in the eyes.

"I did what was right at the time. We were running late." Argued Bankz.

"I know everyone will have an excuse but if you had followed protocol none of this could have happened."

"The man was dead for Christ's sake we had no time to go through the paperwork. We all agreed it was to our best interest to carry the deceased home with us."

"Mr. Bankz don't make it harder that it is. The Vice President want all of you gone by the end of the day. The board of directors feel the same way. If you knew how bad this was you would not open your mouth."

"But Boss. What did we do that could be regarded as gross misconduct?"

Sean's face turned red and wrinkly like a bulldog. He was now fuming with anger, within seconds his eyes had turned red. He stood up and leaned forward touching the table.

"If this comes out you will single handedly destroy this airline with lawsuits and claims. I personally appreciate the work you have done for this airline but your misguided judgment wrote-off that in a flash. You put the lives of the passengers at risk."

Aleck one of the pilots leaned forward.

"With all due respect, I think this is bullshit. You are telling me that after flying for years for you, you just dismiss us like that. I don't think so. Look we were running late. The man died just outside minutes before boarding the plane. We checked the manifest it seemed he was not on the original manifest. Carrying him or leaving him would not have made a significant difference."

Robby got up, one of the pilot.

"Aleck is right assuming he had died after takeoff we still will have had to carry him just like we did. I think there is something you are not telling us."

Sean got up and walked toward the window. He opened the small window and looked outside for a while. He walked back to the table where all the three pilots were now sat down.

"Gentlemen. The case is now a matter of national security. I am afraid I must dismiss you. If you go quietly, you will get your severance packages but any form of resistance will mean you won't get anything."

A buzz sound covered the room as the pilots started talking to each other.

"National security? What do you mean?" Inquired Aleck.

"I can't say much but from what I was told. The man was a bomb?"

Robby got up and looked at Sean with an angry face.

"The on-flight medics checked the deceased he was clean. We did not carry any of his luggage. Everything was left in the tunnel. So, I don't see how he can be classed as a national security issue. If there is something you want to tell us, then tell us now."

"That's all I know for now. This case is classified. If you all leave this will all go away. If you stay and people start questioning all this gentleman, let me warn you this will not end well for you. Any lawsuits and claims by the passengers will do more damage that in turn we will do whatever we can to make sure you feel the heat too. So, gentlemen you are formerly dismissed no matter how harsh this might sound the airline is at risk right now."

Sean got up and walked to the door and opened the door. The three pilots remained sat without knowing what to say.

"Can we talk among us first then decide what we want to do?" Requested Robby.

"Sure, you can but in your own time. Right now, I have some important business call to make."

"It sounds very harsh and disrespectful to us after being loyal to you for all these years."

"Like I said you made a fatal judgmental error. Just imagine if the plane was to explode, and not only that, imagine it being caused by a human error. The most experienced pilots knowingly broke protocol and tried to cover it up and it later turned out that this person had a bomb with him. Just imagine the kind of payouts we could be giving away? That will cripple the airline. Listen to me. Get the packages and take a vacation. Will you? It could be worse and patience is running out as well with the board of directors."

The three men looked at each other and walked toward the door like humbled dogs with tails between their legs. Bankz looked more upset than the other two. He was the senior pilot. The other two relied on his judgment. Over the years, the two were like his protégés, his pupils. He felt single-handedly responsible for all this. The days that followed Bankz felt more and more depressed than the other two. He knew that having been dismissed like that he would find it hard to get a job he liked, which is flying. He started drinking. A new block of flats has just been built in one of the suburban areas. Maureen has just moved in one of the flats. She was one of the first ones to occupy the flats. In her late fifties after her husband died she was alone most of the time. One night she had a dream. In her dream, she was in her village with her late husband. She ran to her husband after hearing the donkey having difficulty breathing.

"Curtis! Curtis, the donkey is choking."

Curtis ran to the donkey pad and found the donkey on its knees having difficulties breathing. Soon after Maureen woke up and heard a female screaming instantly followed but giggling and laughter.

"Damn!"

She cursed covering her head with the pillow. Just next to her flat a couple had just moved in. Katherine and Richard who had recently married had bought one of the newly built flats while saving for a bigger house.

"I can't believe I have so much energy I bet we can do this for hours." Bragged Katherine.

"You know I don't have much time left I have to be at the office by nine o'clock pronto." Explained Richard.

"I have never felt so alive in my life. I bet if we are to have a baby it will be a boy."

The couple were interrupted by the noise as the old lady in the next flat knocked the walls asking the couple to tone it down.

"These walls are like paper walls. I can hear neighbors talking and I bet the neighbors heard me screaming with joy." Alleged Katherine as she burst into laughter slightly embarrassed as well.

"I can't believe time is moving this fast. Darling I must go and take a shower. I have to go to work."

Richard got up and went to take a shower. Months later Richard entered the maternity ward smiling. Katherine was on her hospital bed holding their newly born son.

"He is cute Darling. Our son, our beautiful son." Shouted Richard holding his son in his hands.

The couple were very happy to be blessed with a healthy son. Days later they were at their new home after having sold the flat. Eight years later Katherine and Richard were in their bedroom talking.

"I was called to the school today by Karl's headmaster." Explained Katherine.

"What happened was he in trouble of some kind?" asked Richard worried and concerned about his son.

"He asked me a lot about our son. He said his teacher had complained that he sleeps in the class room. They had raised the issue on more than three occasions."

"It's summer even myself I can't stand the humidity and these elevated temperatures. I think it's common among kids. Is he the only one in his class sleeping during the lessons?"

"As far as they know yes. The head teacher informed me that this has been going on even in winter. But after I explained that we bought him a play-station last Christmas he conceded but insisted that he gets enough sleep."

"So, what did he himself say was the problem?"

"Nothing much he admitted that he was just tired."

"Do you think that maybe we should take him to the doctor for a full checkup?" Enquired Richard.

"I was thinking the same too," replied Katherine.

Weeks later Katherine, Karl and Richard were at the hospital after being referred there by their doctor.

"I truly don't understand why he has to go through this for something that does not require such a procedure," quizzed Richard.

"I was thinking the same thing, but since we have come this far, we might as well let them check him."

The doctor entered the room and sat on his chair after greeting the parents and introducing himself.

"I am doctor Chad I think we need to take bloods of your son to check blood sugar levels and other elements to rule out any diseases. We will need your consent as well to take a small sample of his marrow this will last at max thirty minutes."

"I am not happy about this bone marrow procedure. I swear it's not as bad as you want it to look. We bought a play-station for him but just as a precaution we brought him here. I was not expecting all these operations you are talking about Doctor."

"Don't be alarmed. The operation is a simple procedure. A small hole will be drilled in his hip bone and a sample of his marrow is extracted to be analyzed. The operation is a simple procedure and after half an hour everything will be complete."

"Who will perform the procedure?" Queried Richard worried about his son.

"Unfortunately, I am not one hundred percent sure. We are understaffed it has to be a consultant from another hospital as we don't have anyone available now."

Richard got up and walked toward the window.

"I don't like how it sounds. It's my boy's life we are talking about. What if something goes wrong? He doesn't even know who will be performing the operation. I say no to that. Just do the bloods then we will take it from there."

"What is wrong Darling? This was your idea yourself." Explained Katherine.

"My boy is more stressed up than the first day we came in here and look it has been nearly a week now. I say we take our son home. Forget about the whole thing. We can change the school if that's a big issue. I don't like how this sound."

Richard looked at the doctor and asked to be left alone for the couple to talk.

After nearly half an hour the doctor returned excitedly.

"Good news I spoke to the senior doctor of the hospital who also happened to be the manager. He has assigned a doctor now to carry out the operation but the doctor will be a consultant from another hospital. How does that sound? I am sure that will settle all the concerns you have."

The couple threw each other a quick glance before they agreed. Richard looked a little relaxed. He phoned his family doctor to carry out a background check on this consultant. He turned out to be clean not much was known about him. A week later an SUV packed outside the hospital in the hospital car park. Richard his son and his wife got out of the car and entered the hospital. This was a big day for the family. All the other tests were already completed, and the results were all clear. This was the last test. They were afraid that he was developing a sleeping sickness disease.

"Can I get you something to drink?" Asked Richard getting up and going to the hospital foyer.

"A soda will do. So how long do we have to wait? I thought you said half an hour. It's nearly forty-five minutes now?"

"I will go and check I bet the operation is over now maybe he is still asleep I understand they gave him the anesthetic."

Richard left the hospital foyer and headed toward the operating rooms. He washed his hands and wore hospital gowns before proceeding ahead. He arrived outside the hospital operating room. He looked inside through the big glass windows and instantly he felt sick. He was shocked and frightened by the amount of blood that was on the table and in the doctor's tray. There were a lot of cotton swabs tainted with blood. When the doctor saw Richard through the glass walls standing outside, he panicked and covered his son with a hospital cloth. He looked at the nurse who was standing next to him and with his head pointed at Richard. The nurse quickly walked out and spoke to Richard.

"You shouldn't be here go back and wait in the foyer. We will call you once we are done."

Richard failed to breathe for a while. He felt the worst feeling. He felt like crying. He had let this monster butcher his son on his watch. He felt sick to the bone. He knelt for a while before finding his energies.

"That's my son in there. You said it will take only half an hour. You said a small hole will be drilled to extract the marrow. It seemed you are butchering my son. I want answers right now. What are you doing to my son? That is not what we consented to." Explained Richard with his voice full of anger and dismay.

"Please go and sit down the more you delay me the worse you make the situation. Go back there I will see to it that your son is well and sound."

Richard staggered back and threw himself into the arms of his wife and sobbed.

"What is wrong Darling? Please be strong for our son. Be strong for us. We need you." Sobbed Katherine.

The couple hugged each other for a long time.

"It's just horrendous. It's like this doctor butchered my son. There is so much blood I felt sick. I just couldn't look for the second time."

Both Katherine and Richard sobbed in the foyer. One hour later still there was no news about their son. They both made their way into the operating room. Slowly they peeped inside through the window. Katherine let out a loud scream.

"My son. Darling they killed my son."

The nurse walked out and spoke to the couple.

"The doctor will explain everything in greater detail. We had difficulties operating at the desired position and after some time we operated at a different position and I can say the operation has been a success."

"It looks like you are butchering him why so much blood?"

Asked Richard.

"He has too much fat and we can't operate at the desired place."

The couple looked at each other. The nurse assured them that the operation would be completed soon after, but it took another hour for the couple to see their son by this time the couple were very angry. Richard asked for the badge of the consultant and wrote his name and the hospital he was based. Two hours later precisely one and a half later than the promised time the couple met their son. He looked very disoriented. They stayed with him as he weaned off the anesthetic. The following day they were back home. For the first-time fear constantly knocked their mind's door. Their life changed a lot. This day changed everything. They were never the same again. A huge mistake nearly took out their son. They hoped things will be alright after all.

CHAPTER THREE

Six months later one sunny afternoon Richard received a call from the headmaster of Karl's school. There had been an incident. Karl had collapsed. His body temperature was way high. He was burning. His skin had started to exfoliate like a snakes'. This was very unusual. When Richard touched him he was sure he felt like he was vibrating. Katherine gave him first aid. One early morning Richard after driving for a while turned into the adjacent road and entered the car park. He sat in the car for a while. He looked at the dashboard and closed his eyes for a while. He opened the glove compartment of the car and took out a small box. He adjusted his tie and placed a tie clip. He looked in the rear-view mirror before getting out of the car. He walked nervously but very upset. The automatic doors opened, and he headed straight to the lifts. A female voice could be heard on the PA system from far away. A doorbell rang, and a voice alerted Richard that he was now on level three. The door was about to close again when he placed his hand stopping it from closing. He walked out of the lift and followed the directional arrows before reaching a desk. A receptionist an old woman is sat down going through the Computer system. As soon as Richard nears the desk, the woman lifted her head and removed her reading glasses.

"How can I help you?"

Richard for a while looked everywhere around before looking straight into the receptionist's face.

"I am here to see Dr. Rosen. I have an appointment."

The receptionist looked at the computer screen for a while scrolling down.

"Ah, Mr. Richard please take a seat."

Richard looked at the doctor's office door. The engaged sign was on the door. He looked at his watch and sat down. After ten minutes or so his name was called on the PA system. He looked at his watch and adjusted the clip on his tie and walked to the door. He knocked and entered the room. The female doctor, Dr. Rosen was seated writing something down. Richard sat in the chair in front of the doctor.

"What brings you here Mr. Richard?"

"What did you do to my son? Since the operation, he has never been himself. He vibrates like a damn phone."

"I can't comment on this as I was not in the operating room."

"How can I get hold of the doctor or consultant who carried out the operation? I want all his details."

"I don't know. They sent him at the last minute. We are short of doctors who can carry out this operation so we rely on consultants from other hospitals."

"But still you are responsible for anything that goes wrong. You ordered this operation. You delegated your duties to this consultant but still wholly responsible for the duty of care."

"Mr. Richard how can I be responsible when I was not in the operating room?"

"Still you have a duty of care to find a competent and trustworthy doctor to carry out the operation. The fact that you are denying to providing the details of this consultant is not helping you at all."

"OK I will see what I can do. Let me see if I can get the details of this consultant can you wait outside for a while."

Richard instinctively realized that she knew more than she was admitting to. That made him very upset.

"I suggest you find out the details I want. This is my son we are talking about. Accountability doctor! Ignorance is not an excuse. My son's life is in your hands."

The doctor looked shocked she never expected to hear this from Richard. Richard knew that this could only be the tip of the iceberg. The fact that she tried to cover for this doctor only raised suspicion to her involvement. Richard got up and walked out back into the foyer. He felt betrayed. The operation was not necessary. He had put his son's life in danger. He wished he can wake up and find that all this was just a dream. He was busy thinking about his son when his phone rung sending him flying.

"Hello Darling are you okay?"

Katherine was crying on the other end uncontrollably.

"What is wrong.?" Inferred Richard.

"Darling. It's our son." Sobbed Katherine.

"What's wrong."

"He just collapsed."

"What do you mean just collapsed check if he is breathing?"

Richard got up and walked left and right in the foyer.

"He is breathing, but he is throwing a fit. I just checked his eyes the pupil has disappeared."

The door suddenly opened, and the doctor stood at the door.

"Mr., Richard you can come back in."

Richard looked at the doctor but continued talking on the phone. Richard was about to leave the doctor's office when his wife mentioned that their son had woken up and seemed to be feeling better. Richard looked at his watch. A good twenty minutes had passed. He walked to the doctor's office and entered the office. He sat down and looked at the doctor who was writing something down. The doctor stretched her arm and handed Richard a small piece of paper. Richard got the paper and quickly looked at it.

"What is this?" Asked Richard.

The doctor did not reply at first but instead looked at Richard.

"$2000!! Is the money you owe this hospital Mr. Richard."

"But you told me the bill was covered by my insurance."

"The consultation fees and any prescriptions, yes but not the operation itself."

"The operation was not necessary. I had insisted that it was not necessary, but you insisted that it was necessary and now you come and talk about this bill. I swear if you don't take me seriously I will sue you and the hospital. I came for the details of the consultant who carried out the operation. The damage he has done is more than the $2000 you are asking from me. Accountability doctor. We all must pay for our actions. No one is immune. So, I ask again where are the details of this consultant. This is my son we are talking about."

"By the way how is your son?"

Richard stopped talking and looked at the doctor with sharp eyes. He looked confused. The doctor had clearly said this in a cunning and boastful way.

"Excuse me?"

"I said how is your son?

"My son?"

"I want you to take me seriously too. You owe the hospital $2000. Pay that money now then we can talk about anything else." Said the doctor folding her arms and sitting comfortably in the chair.

"So, you know about this? You are responsible for this? Are you blackmailing me? Are you sure you are putting my son through all that for bloody $2000?"

Richard got up and walked toward the office window. He looked outside and saw police cars just arriving and officers with guns getting out of the cars quickly and into the building. He appeared as if nothing had happened and walked back to his chair.

"Mark my words doctor. Accountability. We are all going one day to be asked to pay for our actions. My son can't go through all this just because of a $2000 hospital bill. That's the lowest and most cruel form of blackmail. You put money first than my son's life I promise you justice shall be served one day."

Richard got up and walked toward the door.

"Don't go stay I will ring someone and see if they can give me the details."

Richard looked at his watch and aimed the tie clip at the doctor and left. Quickly he looked at the lift's floor indicator and noticed that the lifts were heading up. He took the stairs and ran as fast as he can downstairs. Quickly he entered his car. He had just started the car engine when he felt the most excruciating pain on the back of his head. Two hours later Richard woke up with a heavy head and blurred eyes sight. He looked around and heard the voice he had heard before on the PA system calling for a one doctor. He touched his neck and felt drying blood on his neck. He looked at his hands. Above in the corner was a camera with a red flashing light. He tried to get up but felt very heavy. Minutes later two men entered the room and dragged him out to another room after blindfolding him.

"What are you doing? Where are you taking me?"

Richard struggled, but he felt a sharp piercing on his neck. The next time he came around he was surrounded by seven people. He looked around looking at all the people. There were three females and the rest men.

"Mr. Richard have you ever abused your son?"

"How would you best describe your sexuality?"

"How is your relationship with your wife?"

Richard felt like the world was falling apart on him.

"Where is my son and my wife? Who are you? What have you done to me?"

"Just answer these questions and you will be on your way home before you know it.!"

"I am not answering any questions. To hell with all you motherfuckers. I am going now."

Richard tried to get up but somehow, he felt weak. He staggered a little and slumped back in his chair.

"What did you do to me? I will damn sue you."

"What is the relationship with your wife like?"

"Fuck you! None of your business."

"Have you ever abused your son?"

"You ask me that question again I swear you will need a straw after I am finished you with. Let me go right now. You evil cowards. You use my son to blackmail me. He is only eight years. Just because of $2000. If I were God, I would make sure that all of you pay for this. You are telling me that you torture my son so you remain in your job? Why can't you change your job and stop all this?"

"This institution was established long before you were born and will still be here after you have died. So, have you ever abused your son?"

"In other words, you mean where is our $2000?"

"We don't care about your money. We can get that money anytime we want."

"He is only eight years old. I swear whatever it is, it is not an act of God. It's purely human man made. You understand me? It's unspeakable daylight robbery. What for? I don't get you. So, you maintain your job? Do you know how many people are suffering needless just because you must have a job? God created everyone so they enjoy life for most of the time but you think otherwise. My son is in pain needless every day. There is no day that passes without your tampering. If I were God, I would kill all of you and all your family in cold blood. That way you will understand how wrong this feels. That way you will understand. That way you will take me seriously. You might have done this several times before but I tell you, this time you have marked the wrong man. My son will never go through this just you have a job and something to talk about. Hell no. We came for help and not to be subjected to torture."

A tear rolled down on Richard's left cheek.

Silence broke out.

"What a moving speech Mr. Richard we have heard all this before honestly it's boring as if you are going to do anything about this. If I were you, I would be coughing up the money you owe the hospital right now."

"I can write a check now but that is not the point. You tampered with my son's system. The problems you are causing are more and I can sue you and this hospital."

"If you want to see a Judge twitching and throwing a fit, then be my guest."

"So, you know? So, it's true it's you making my son vibrate? I swear I am going to kill all of you. He is an innocent boy. He will never harm even a fly."

"Yes, we know that but you will."

"Me!?"

"Why?"

"Don't ask me to repeat myself. Have you ever abused your son?"

"Why you ask that?"

"We have reasons to believe that he is showing signs of abuse."

"He plays the play-station all the time he sleeps less than the other kids that's all. All this is bullshit you know that."

One of the female attendants overturned the page of the file she was holding.

"Your wife implied that you might have abused your son."

"This is bullshit let me go right now. I swear you will regret this. You caused too much damage already let me go and I will forget about all this as long as my son is okay."

"Your wife suggested that your son smelled sperms when she carried out the first aid."

Richard felt a huge lump moving in his heart. He did not answer this female instead he cut her into pieces with his eyes only if eyes would cut. The other female attendant joined the conversation.

"We have reason to believe that your son is running away from home and behaving like this because you are abusing him."

Richard tried getting up but felt all his energies drained.

"You all sit here as if nothing had happened and pretending to not know what had happened when this doctor had abused my son and now trying to cover up everything."

"Let me get this straight. You are saying that all this is happening because you believe this doctor did something to your son. Please be real. Doctors are to help people not actually cause problems in people. Are you taking any medication? Are you an alcoholic?"

"You damn dog. You have the guts to accuse me of all that when you actually know what they are doing to my son."

"Are you having problems sleeping? Have you suffered from depression in the past?"

Richard looked down for a while. He searched his pockets and found that his car keys and phone were missing.

"Where is my phone? Where are my car keys?"

"All taken for safe keeping. You will get back all these after the meeting."

"How can a human being vibrate unless you have tampered with his system?"

"He might have been sitting in a room when something heavy like a lorry or train was passing by."

"He was in his room. I was there with him?"

"Who else was there with you? Did your wife witness this too?"

"Not really but that does not mean that it didn't happen."

"What else is strange about his behavior?"

"How can a young boy smell sperms?"

"That's the main reason we called you here? How is your sexual relationship with your wife?"

"You double faced low life dog. You imply something like that again and God knows what I will do to you." The male attendant dragged his chair forward.

"So, is that the way you feel about women as low life dogs?"

"You damn smart ass scum bag trying to set me up. He is my son! Was your mother a whore you ask that kind of question?" Queried Richard furious.

"My mother a whore no. Why you ask that?" Questioned the male attendant.

"If you were born from a loving mother and you were raised properly, you would not even ask me that question."

"Okay, I will rephrase. Are you homosexual?"

"Homosexual or not that has nothing to do with this. This doctor thinks she can get away with this? They tampered with my son."

"I think you are experiencing a nervous breakdown. Everything you are suggesting is just absurd."

"My son had an operation here at the hospital."

"So, what, that can't prove anything."

"This doctor somehow tampered with my son's system. They might have put something inside."

The other male attendant took the doctors reports and went through them.

"There is nothing in these reports that you reported any problems within the first three months of the operation."

"We didn't notice anything until after seven months. I rang this doctor several times, but she refused to talk over the phone."

"As far as the reports are concerned the operation was successful."

"It took more than two hours for an operation that normally take twenty minutes. Don't you think that he had enough time to do more than he confessed as having had done. This is not any help. This is abuse at its worst level. I say the doctor had more time to do more harm than he is admitting to."

"Are you crazy Mr. Richard? Doctors always do good and never harm patients."

"I think you know more than you are admitting here. In that case, I refuse to talk to you. Give me my phone, car keys and wallet now. I write you a check and go."

One of the females got up and brought back a small box and placed this in front of Richard. Richard took out his wallet and his check book he wrote a check for two thousand dollars and staggered up and out of the building. Disoriented he headed to the parking lot. He stopped and looked around. There were now three identical cars to his. He walked to the one he knew was his. He tried to open the door, but the door did not open. He stopped and thought for a while. He had a quick flashback of the time he had arrived. Surely, he had parked there. He looked at the keys and pressed the remote key. A beeping sound and flashing amber lights from the car on the other side of the car park caught his attention. He stopped for a while and looked around. He saw a camera turning around and pointing at him. He stretched his middle finger and pointed at the camera. He staggered to his car and entered the car. He drove off harsh braking here and there. After driving for a while he stopped and parked his car. He took out his phone and dialed a taxi. He waited for a taxi and when the taxi was nearby a car appeared from nowhere and four men jumped out.

"You are under arrest for dangerous driving while intoxicated."

"What fuck off from me. I am waiting for a taxi. In fact, there is my taxi."

"We don't care get in the car right now."

"Over my dead body, you bastards. I am going home to see my son right now."

Richard staggered toward the taxi. The four men struggled with Richard for a while before he knew it Richard was on the ground. The last thing he remembered was seeing a big black shoe in front of his nose.

"All rise Judge Evans presiding." shouted the court's usher as the Judge entered the court. Everyone in the court stood up. The Judge seated in his chair and ordered everyone to sit down. The Judge looked at the prosecuting attorney. A woman in her mid-thirties smartly dressed up with a strong voice that did not match her body stood up and walked in front of the jury.

"Today our freedom and rights have been impinged. Our way of life is at risk. God gave every man and women the right to live freely and choose what's right for him or her. To choose what is right for his son or daughter for that matter. Freedom to do what you want when you want. Freedom to privacy and rights to a peaceful life. But as you will hear throughout the court, these doctors took the law into their own hands and decided that they were like God they can tell us how we should live our own lives without our consent. These doctors are worse than anyone in the history of mankind. If it was for the good of mankind, at least some of this would make sense but this is their way of controlling the people extorting money whenever they feel like. Blackmailing the innocent law-abiding citizens making the otherwise strong people weak to control the people. There are more than twenty charges brought against them. I will name the ones that are fundamental to this case. They have breached human rights to freedom and rights to choose and make their own decisions. They have been accused of forcing patients abusing them for hours. They are accused of misleading cheating and swindling patient's into giving up their life savings. They are accused of infringing human rights to privacy as I will show later. They are accused of drugging patients without their consent. They are accused of murder as they are tampering with the person's system in most cases resulting in death. They are accused of causing unnecessary suffering among patients so that they keep themselves in a job. They are accused of cruel degrading acts which I will explain later as we go along. They are charges of robbing their patients. They are charges of grievous bodily harm as others were literally burned and cooked alive. The victims describe these doctors as worse than the murders. I will show you that no matter what excuse they are going to give for such horrendous acts all this amounts to gross abuse and torture unheard of only in the medieval times. This practice might have been okay in that time but my question to you is this. Do you think this is appropriate in modern day when we have gadgets and watches to wake us up? When we have books computers and so forth to help us plan and remind us of all the important things we require. Before the technological error, then maybe but now this amounts to needless abuse at a scale never witnessed before. The values are changing the world is changing. Only lawsuits and claims will put an end to this practice. Only lawsuits and claims will make them understand that this is wrong. For all these years, no one has been able to document this at such a level that it was impossible to bring a successful claim. I hope this case will be the test case that will not only see an end to this evil practice in the name of help but the drying up of all their financial sources as well. We want a comprehensive approach on this matter. I say it's easy for them to carry out such hideous practices because they have a wider source of money. Which if we are to scrutinize this too you will see that the money is obtained through blackmail threatening to kill and in some cases killing people? A comprehensive approach will put an end to this. Imagine living in a world where your son grow up free from diseases and any deformities. Imagine a world where your son will grow up without fear of being abused daily so that someone have a good enough patient attendant. A world where only God decides when and how you will die. A world where money or no money you will still enjoy life. A world where no one tells you what you will eat or what you will do. I am free and I have the right to make my own decisions good or bad still it's my choice. Ladies and gentlemen, I guarantee you that you will hear defense stories that they had you in mind but I say this to you that they are no better that say the murderers out there. No better than drug dealers. No better than pimps out there. This is rearing and grooming at the highest level. These are people we are talking about not chickens or poultry that can be treated in this way. Its abuse at an unprecedented level. You will hear defense stories that they were doing this for us. That they had us in mind. That they were concerned about our wellbeing but the picture now emerging is totally different. This is a money business at the highest levels with murders, privacy infringement, kidnapping, illegally drugging patients, blackmailing and daylight robbery. This is all systematized and institutionalized that it can't be separated from the society itself. But today and all the days that are following I am going to prove that these accused doctors are no better than the murders, the rapists, the loan sharks and all the scums of the society. Some might say not everyone is like that but how do we know this is not what all of them do? Even in the lightest scenario this is the case of a bad egg that spoils all. To stop it is to apply a comprehensive program that will cut off sources of funding, any support and very stiff punishment to the accused. This is not a light matter as they have accused my client of suffering a nervous breakdown when they know that this is really happening. They will not stop at anything. Until you are in the shoes of my client, you will never see the impact and consequences of their actions. Trust me, they have answers for everything. They have cover-ups everywhere but when can we say enough is enough. There is money out there. You can tell me that the world is still the same it was say in the 17 centuries. Gone are the days when we burn someone first then apologies or try to prove how good we are at correcting our mistakes. Accountability starts now. We should all be accountable for our actions and that includes these doctors and the institutions covering their tracks."

CHAPTER FOUR

The defending lawyer a man in his late forties well dressed up rose from his chair after the prosecuting lawyer has sat down. He looked at everyone in the court and stopped for a while. He looked at the accused doctors.

"I was very fortunate to have had a very good family doctor. We have known our doctor as far as we can remember. In fact, my father and his granddad had generations after generations of doctors from the same family. To me he is more than a doctor. He is a friend. A very special family doctor. Don't get me wrong some doctors are killer doctors but it's in the worst scenarios. The counsel is implying that because of one rotten egg all of them are now spoiled but I strongly disagree with that. I have looked at all cases where the doctor ended up abusing his patient. The patients themselves had made it easy for that doctor to abuse them. In the case of the accuser he clearly tried to rob the hospital of $2000. Hospitals are now like businesses they must make a profit or cover its cost to remain functional. The accuser abused the hospital and think he can get away with this. God somehow saw this, and the accuser suffered a nervous breakdown before he was questioned about the hospital fees not after as he claimed. I will show that having failed to pay the hospital bill the accuser then refused to pay the money and instead accused the doctor who helped his son of tampering with his son's system. I want to make it clear that these doctors did not go and look for the accuser but instead the accuser went to the hospital when his son was not feeling well. Unfortunately, things did not go as planned but that can't make my clients accountable and responsible for all these problems. It is with sad regrets that the accused suffered all this but I say this had nothing to do with my clients. All these accusations are not justified. I will argue that the accuser with regret lost his son and because of grief now is accusing my clients. It is with much sadness that the accuser's son ended up dead in mysterious circumstances but I would argue that that had nothing to do with my clients."

Richard looked at everyone in the court before feeling the strong grip made by his wife Katherine. He looked at her and he saw tears and pain in her eyes. He looked at the doctors and saw them with this happy cunning face. He looked away from his wife hiding tears in his left eye. He had tried very hard to conceal the pain he was feeling but a drop of his tear on his wife's hand sold him out. He looked at the defending attorney. He felt sick. Surely, he was just as bad as them if not worse in the sense that he cunningly made them look cool. If it were him who had lost a son surely, he might not be grinning as he was doing sat there. After lunch, the court resumed, and the accused doctor was seating in the defended box. The other accused defendant was sat in the chairs on the defendant's side. The doctor looked calm and unconcerned. He kept looking at his watch. This was a waste of his precious time. To him this was just like any other day. People die every day, to him he didn't see the need for all this drama. What was so special about this boy? I guess he wondered. The prosecuting attorney rose from her seat and walked toward the defendant. She looked at him first before walking to her desk. She opened a file and looked at the picture in the file before walking back toward the defendant.

"So, we can say with much certainty that you are the doctor who operated on the accuser's son before he died. Yes or No."

"Yes."

"How long does it take to carry out the operation?"

"On average twenty to thirty minutes."

Diana the prosecuting attorney walked back to her desk. She took a report and walked toward the doctor.

"Look at this report. Is this your signature did you sign this report?"

The doctor took his reading glasses from his pocket and wore them. He looked attentively at the report. With much confidence and certainty, he replied.

"Yes, it's my signature. Yes, I signed this report."

Your Honor and members of the jury I will present exhibit one. This is a report written by the doctor after the operation.

"Can you tell the court what time is written on the report as time it took to carry out the operation?"

The doctor looked at the report closely.

"Two hours forty minutes."

"But in your own words you said this operation can last between twenty and thirty minutes. Can you explain that?"

"There were complications. The son had too much fat in the area I was supposed to operate."

"By complications does that mean you might also have caused damaged? Has this happened before?"

"No. No. This was the first time."

"Is that not correct that it took more minutes than usual because you did more damage than you thought?"

"No I carried the operation perfectly."

"But you said you had problems that he had fat why is that not in the report?"

"I didn't think that was important."

"Is it not possible that you might have tampered with his own system, damaged a nerve or something?"

"It's not possible."

"Is it not true that you inserted some remote operated instrument instead of just extracting blood.?"

The doctor did not answer.

The defending lawyer Silverdale stood up.

"Objection your Honor the counsel is intimidating the defended and assuming facts not in evidence."

"Counsel be careful where you are going with this."

"I will rephrase your honor."

"Yes or no. If it were just taking the blood, you could have finished in no time than the two hours forty minutes stipulated."

"Probably."

"Just answer yes or no. Is it true that two hours forty minutes is a long enough time to have damaged some nerves or inserted some objects as alleged by my client?"

The doctor remained quiet.

"I repeat is two hours forty minutes enough time for someone to have carried out what my client alleged? Answer the question god-damn-it!"

The prosecuting attorney shouted at the operating doctor as she was now fuming with anger and frustrations. The doctor remained silent. The prosecuting attorney Diana walked very fast to her desk and took a report and gave it to the doctor.

"Look at the photos and tell the court which operation is synonymous with this scar or wound!"

The doctor looked at the photo but did not say anything.

"Doctor the operation you carried out where on the body is it normally carried out on."

"A small hole in the hip bone."

"Did you operate on the hip bone?"

"Yes, I guess so. That was a long time ago."

"Doctor look at the report you wrote and tell me where you carried out the operation."

The doctor looked worried for the first time and hesitated to reply.

"Diana hit the table sending some papers flying. Tell me right now where did you operate on the body."

"It is written here that on the lumbar."

"You are telling me and the court that you mistake the hip bone and operated on the lumbar region?"

"Like I said he had too much fat on the hip bone and I operated on the lumbar."

"So, you are telling the court that you risked damaging his nerves and operated somewhere else than his father had consented to."

A buzz sound filled the court as everyone started talking to each other.

"I will have silence in court." Ordered the Judge.

"He had lost a lot of blood and I had to operate on him very fast."

"Why you didn't mention all this in the report?"

"I guess I didn't think that was important."

"What did you think was not important then? Getting a consent? Damaging nerves and causing excessive bleeding? What exactly did you not think was important?"

"Objection the counsel is speculating instead of relying on facts."

"Your honor I will show the court that the doctor is a calculating and manipulative crook. He says only what suits him and not what is important. You have heard from him that some things we might think that are of grave concern to us are simply things that are not important to him. In that regard, I think it's open to me to try to deduce from all the information what exactly happened that day, his views and his credibility."

"True or false that the lumbar region is the most sensitive area and dangerous area of the body to operate."

"True."

"So, without consent you took things in your own hands and still carried out the procedure."

"Objection your Honor the counsel is leading my client."

"Your owner the doctor accused my client of suffering a nervous breakdown when he not only misled everyone but also lied and tried to cover it. In that matter, whatever he said should be treated with suspicion."

"Overruled. You may continue."

"Is it normal for a human being to vibrate?"

"No."

"Is it normal for a young boy of eight years to smell sperms in his breath?"

"Unheard of but why not ask his father that question?"

A huge buzz sound covered the whole court as people started whispering to each other.

"Silence in court." Ordered the Judge.

"Is it not true that this started after the operation either you botched the operation as my client alleges or that it is true you placed a device you are using to redirect sperms to where they should not be? Answer yes or no."

"I would not be blamed for his father's perverting acts. He is the bend one. He is the one you should be asking that."

"Did my client owed you or the hospital any money at any time?"

"After the operation, he disappeared he thought he can get away with this."

"I repeat did my client owed the hospital any money?"

"Yes $2000."

"I read the leaflet at the time he consented to the operation to be carried out on the hip it is stated that the medical insurance will cover for everything."

"Yes, but you have to read the small print otherwise we won't be making money.?"

"Does that not amount to misrepresentation or cheating my client? Was my client informed about this."

"Yes, he should have been informed my duty is to carry out the operation and not to discuss insurance policies."

"So, is it not true that you avoided operating on the hip bone that was covered by the insurance and choose to operate on the lumbar which was not covered by the insurance rendering my client's insurance invalid?"

The doctor looked at the other doctors especially the senior female doctor. As if asking her if he can answer yes or no.

"Damn it! Answer the question. Did you deliberately operated on the lumbar region to get my client in debt to blackmail and experiment on his son?"

Diana was very angry this time. The doctor was not taking everyone seriously. People had come to realize that these doctors pose more health risks than they solve. A young boy had died. The hospital was arrogant that Diana's client had abused the system by not paying for the hospital operation. But Diana was sure they played dirty games to get him indebted to them without knowing there by blackmailing him and justifying experimenting on his son. When he confronted them, they accused him of abusing his own son to damage his credibility and separating the couple before killing his son.

"Your honor and ladies and gentlemen of the jury. This doctor although we don't know now that he acted alone, or that this was not common hospital practice to abuse the trust placed in him by his patient. He went on to operate without the consent.

The consent given was for operating on the hip bone. He went on to operate on the most sensitive and dangerous part of the body without my client's consent. Him as the doctor knew that the insurance would not cover operations done there because we are talking of $millions of claims and compensation if something goes wrong, if the doctor damages nerves in that region. Operating in this area is more riskier and was not covered by the insurance my client had. That would invalidate my client's insurance and thereby give the doctors an upper hand as they will set up my client and blame it on none payment of hospital fees. I am going to prove that this was not a mistake or the circumstances leading to his son's death. This was a pre-planned calculated plan by this doctor to abuse and abuse again my client's son until the day he died and indirectly causing his death. Had this doctor sort consent my client would have never agreed for the operation to go on. This was just a routine check-up and this leading to his death is just unjustified and amounts to first degree murder."

At this moment in time it started to sink in for the doctor that one way or the other soon justice will catch up with him.

"Your honor and members of the jury. I am going to prove to you that this doctor will not stop at anything. After butchering my client's son, he went on to drug my client and falsely imprisoned him and started a tirade of a campaign against my client with the help of the council who he donated the money to which he raised from my client. The doctor started a campaign aimed at degrading treatment toward my client calling him names and somehow tampering with his son's system to look like he has been abusing his son. After all this, this doctor came to court with never seen before arrogance and continue to lie in front of the jury. But I tell you this justice has caught up with him and all his accomplices."

The defending attorney Silverdale stood up after a while. He pushed his hair backward sand pulled up his trousers. He did his jacket and walked toward the doctor he was defending.

He stood in front of his box and looked at him.

"It is with much regret that a young life was abruptly taken away from us. It is with great sadness that we lost a young boy in such circumstances. Ladies and gentlemen of the jury and your honor all this had nothing to do with my client and as things are he can't be responsible for things that happened after three months let alone six months. He is exercising his rights. All the evidence presented so far is just circumstantial. This is a serious matter but please vibrating people? It's unheard of. For some the loss of a loved one is so unbearable that they start imagining things. All these stories about kidnapping and drugging by my client are all circumstantial. This is the mind of a man who has experienced enough trauma. When someone losses a close loved one it makes, them feel better if they blame someone. My client was recommended by the senior doctor at the hospital. They trusted him to carry out the job successfully. His track record speaks more for him than anything else."

Silverdale walked in front of the jury.

"Members of the jury no matter how sad this might be my client has done nothing wrong. He carried out the operation to the best of his abilities given the circumstances. This also explains the time it took to carry out the operation."

Silverdale walked toward the doctor and stood in front of him.

"Is it a widespread practice that sometimes though in rare circumstances an operation can be carried out on the lumbar region instead of on the hip?"

"Yes."

"In best of your knowledge could the operation have been performed better?"

"No. That is the best one can do given the circumstances."

"No further questions."

Silverdale walked and sat in his chair in the defended corner.

Diana remained seated. Everyone else looked at her.

"When you had, difficulties operating on the hip why didn't you stop and seek consent first before continuing?"

"I didn't think this was necessary I had consent."

"Is it true that you had consent to operate on the hip only?"

"Yes."

"Why then proceed to the lumbar without consent?"

"I assumed it was implied consent?"

"So, are you telling me that operating on the hip and the lumbar made no difference?"

"Yes. Made no difference at all."

"If that is the case why were they not covered by the insurance if in your eyes, it was the same.?"

A buzzing noise filled the court room.

"Silence in court please be quiet." Ordered the Judge.

"I ask you again. If it was the same in your eyes why then the hospital billed him a $2000 bill?"

The doctor did not reply he looked at the other doctors.

"Did you carry out the operation on the lumbar without consent answer yes or no?"

"No."

"I will rephrase. Were you given consent to operate on the lumbar region by the father of the deceased? Answer Yes or no."

"Consent was implied."

"Damn it. Answer yes or no." Shouted Diana hitting the table with her palm.

The doctor refused to answer.

"Objection your honor counsel is antagonizing my client." Shouted Silverdale.

"Counsel can you approach my bench." Ordered the Judge.

"Where are you going with this? Trade carefully." Suggested the Judge.

"Your honor it is open to me to establish if the doctor performed an illegal operation without consent and as such then my client could be telling the truth that he tampered with my client's son's system or in the worst-case scenario deliberately damaged my client's nerves. Therefore, guilty of murder."

"OK overruled but trade careful."

"Doctor did you have consent to operate on the lumbar?"

"Yes."

"Why then did the insurance refuse to cover this kind of operation?"

"Did you inform my client at any time that you might operate on the lumbar?"

"No."

"So why are you sure you were given the consent? Is it correct to say you assumed you had the consent when in fact you didn't have the consent?"

"Probably."

"Ladies and gentlemen this is one manipulative doctor. It is clear no consent was given yet this doctor insisted that there was implied consent. The fact that the insurance refused to cover for this operation clearly indicates that a separate written consent was needed before carrying out the procedure. Because of this operation my client's son ended up dead. I would say the doctor was responsible as this operation set up a chain of events leading to his death."

Diana walked to her desk and took out some documents. She looked at the documents.

"Have you ever carried out this operation before?"

"Yes." Replied the doctor.

"Do you know what happened to the last person you operated on?"

"I don't know."

"Ladies and gentlemen of the jury. This is not the first time someone has complained about this doctor. In fact, he was transferred after a patient sued the hospital after a botched operation. You will be astonished to find out that he operated on the lumbar again resulting in strange behavior leading to a horrific accident."

The court went wild and everyone started talking to each other.

"Order in court." Advised the doctor.

"Were you forced to transfer because you botched an operation just like in this case?"

"No."

"Let me refresh your mind. Were you forced to transfer from your old job?"

"It was mutual. I wanted to move on."

"Is it correct to say that you were offered a transfer instead of being dismissed just because there was a shortage of doctors who could perform this kind of operation."

"That's not correct."

"What happens when a patient successfully sued the hospital? Is that not admittance of guilty? A fact that the doctor was guilty. Why did the hospital ended up paying the patients?"

"It was not a payment as such. This was a refund?"

"What do you mean? In the documents, it's written that it was a compensatory award."

"The insurance initially refused to cover for the operation. The patient was asked to pay instead which he did from his savings. The insurance then later accepted to include the operation as one of those it covered. It later sent a check. The hospital later decided to refund the patient his money."

"Was this before or after he sued the hospital?"

"After he sued."

"Why did he sue the hospital?"

"He was crazy if you ask me."

"Ladies and gentlemen, the first claimant complained about the same issues as raised by my client. After the operation, he started having unexplained issues and as in the report just like in this case. This doctor took more time than he promised. He operated without consent as well. He too complained of vibrating and having difficulties with his sight that resulted in an accident causing serious injuries. He went on to successfully sue the hospital."

"No, he did not. The hospital gave him his money back after the insurance paid out." Explained the doctor.

"Why would the hospital admit that this was a compensatory payout?" Asked Diana.

"This was just for publicity. Now you understand why they couldn't sake me."

"You mean they just could not prove it?"

"Objection counsel is speculating without concrete evidence."

"Sustained paraphrase." Ordered the Judge.

"No further questions your honor."

Diana sat down and looked at Richard and Katherine. Later that day Diana, Richard and Katherine were outside the court talking. They shook hands and Diana headed to her car while Richard and Katherine entered their car and drove off.

"I feel hurt. It was all my fault I should have just dropped it when he first refused. I should have listened to my son. He could still be alive with us."

"I cry myself to sleep. I feel like I have been robbed yet they try to cover up all this and make it look as if that's OK. You too you just sit there."

"What do you mean? You think I don't feel the pain you are feeling too." Asked Richard.

"You just look when he is calling our son crazy yet we know they were tampering with his system until the day he died."

"What should I do? They are all crooks. They are all in this together. Have you seen how they try to cover up everything?"

"They must pay. They smile and boast about how successful the operation was when my son is being eaten by the worm's underneath. I despise you too.

You side with them. The fact that you just sat there when you know they were all lying makes it worse. I despise them. I swear by my son one day I revenge."
"What did you expect me to do? Shoot them?"
"Yes. They shot our son. What do you call that? Did you see how he died? Maybe you need reminding too."
"We lost enough I don't want anything to happen to us."
"What's left of us? You tell me? Without my boy life will never be the same. So, what is left of this family?"
"Us I have you we can start again."
"Start again so they rob us again. Hell no. If you don't fight for my son, forget it. I will never give you another one because they will still take away from us as they please. You are not the man I married. You know that somehow, they pretended they were helping. Parading in front of everyone as if this is right. That doctor abused my son. He murdered my son and you think this is okay. I would rather die with my son than let this too faced scum bag tell the entire world that they were helping him when they were murdering him. Show that you love me. Show that you love my son and fight for us do something."
"Darling I took them to court let the court decide."
"Do you think that it's just him involved? All the top doctors and managers are 100% behind him you can't sense the arrogance? Tomorrow you will hear the manager do everything to cover for him. You saw our son there is no doubt they were tampering with his system."
"That's what I said in the first place."
"So, why stick by them? Maybe it's true what they were saying about you."

Before Katherine even finished talking Richard slapped her in the face with an open arm. She screamed and yelled at Richard.
"You bastard one day my brothers will beat you up. I lost my son and you are turning against me."
Richard stopped the car and hugged Katherine very tight for a while.
"Richard. Richard,"
"What?"
"I can't breathe."
"Oh sorry. I just want you to know that I love you. Sorry I just lost it for a while. I meant no harm. I never abused anyone let alone my son. He was my boy my own flesh and blood. I swear they tampered with his system. They tried to set me up. You should believe me."
"I apologize too. I should never have said something like that."
"Come my love let's go tomorrow another big day in court."

CHAPTER FIVE

A cat crossed the road into a nearby park. It sniffed
here and there before escaping through an opening
into the nearby yard. It looked around and saw a lot
of cars parked in the car park. Suddenly the big
wooden door opened. A man came outside and lit his
cigarette. He started smoking. He looked at the cat
and started whispering something before blowing
smoke into the cat's face. The cat escaped ending up
banging on the car tires as smoke blinded its eyes.
The man walked back into the court and sat in the
members of the public area. Silverdale was smartly
dressed up as usually. He was well built with a big
stomach which he supported with cross-belts. He was
laid back. In everything he did there was no any
urgency. It seemed he had a good grip of the world
and all the surrounding people. His face spoke of
confidence and good organization. He was the
symbol of the modern-day man. Relaxed and calm yet
good at everything he did. In the defendant's box a

woman in her late fifties sat in the chair. She looked more professional and unconcerned about all this. She frowned here and there as if this was just a waste of her time.

"All rise the honorable Judge Campbell presiding. The court is now in session." Announced the usher.

"All be seated." Ordered the Judge.

Silverdale did not waste time. He stood up and walked toward the defendant.

"How would you describe the doctor?"

"Objection irrelevant." Shouted Diana.

"Your honor I need to establish credibility and character."

"Objection overruled."

"You may answer the question."

"He acts professionally, a really good doctor."

"Good, that you will recommend him even now to carry any operation?" Enquired Silverdale.

"Absolutely."

"Is it common to operate on the lumbar area when you can't extract marrow from the hip bone?"

"Yes, as long as consent is given."

"Is it not true also that in risk operations like this there is implied consent in case something bad happens and further treatment or operation is needed to save a life?"

"Yes, it's true as long as there is communication."

"Ladies and gentlemen. I want to state that my client spoke to the father of the deceased the first time he had problems operating on the hip bone. This was confirmed by the nurse who was with my client because of this my client assumed he had been given consent and went on to operate on his son."

"In your opinion was there any wrong doing done?"

"I can't answer that question for sure because I was not in the operating room."

"Looking at the evidence before you what would you say? Was the operation carried out professionally?"

"Yes."

"No further questions."

Silverdale went to sit down.

Diana went through a lot of documents first before getting up.

"What is your position at the hospital?"

"I am the senior doctor as well as the manager."

"In this case do you think that there should have been explicit consent for operating on the lumbar region?"

"Yes, but it just depends like I said I was not in the operating room."

"Are you aware that similar allegations were brought up at his old hospital against him?"

"I wasn't aware but I am aware now."

"Now that you know do you think you used good judgment in delegating tasks to him."

"I think like he said the hospital accepted liability as a goodwill gesture and in that regard, I think I made a good decision in appointing him to perform the operation,"

"Are you aware that two people have complained about this doctor but all complaining about the same thing and in all cases resulting in death or serious injuries?"

"Yes."

"Would that not make you think that the doctor is dangerous?"

"He is a good doctor. People die after operations and they will still continue to do so."

"What about this insurance scam? Operating on the lumbar not covered by the insurance then later demand money? Is this a way the hospital is raising money nowadays?"

"No comment."

"If you were the father of the murdered son."

"Objection counsel is leading my client. The son died in an accident he was not murdered."

"Sustained. Rephrase." Ordered the Judge.

"If your son had died in these circumstances would you not sue the hospital and the doctor?"

"I am not in the shoes of the accuser and I would not like to speculate."

"My client is arguing that murder charges should be brought up to you as well."

"What did I do wrong. I was not in the operating room."

"Accountability doctor. You owe my client and his son a duty of care. He came to you and you delegated to someone else and his son ended up dead and so you are responsible."

A buzzing sound of people talking covered the court. The Judge this time did not order silence. He let the people talk for a while. After a while instantly there was silence again.

"This doctor ladies and gentlemen of the jury owe a duty of care. She delegated her task but still accountable for any wrong doing. The first hospital admitted because the senior doctor or manager was accountable and responsible for whatever this junior doctor did on her behalf. This could explain why they choose to transfer him instead of firing him. I want to argue that this doctor is responsible for the death of my client's son. The junior doctor was carrying out tasks delegated to him. We want to bring up charges of incompetent and poor judgment on part of this senior doctor. It was open to her to do a thorough background check of this junior doctor. If she had done that at least she should have known his short comings and try to prevent this from happening again. I think she was aware but ignored this. Let me remind the court that ignorance is not an excuse. If she had been concerned about the duty of care, then she would have done everything in her power to safeguard the safety of my client's son."

Diana paused for a while.

"This doctor's actions led to a serious accident and now the death of an innocent boy. The hospital knew and tried to cover this up by smearing my client which nearly caused him a nervous breakdown. My client might have suffered a nervous breakdown, but it was because of the trauma my client experienced after the botched operation. It was clear this doctor tampered somehow with his son's system or and that he might have damaged his nerves. He operated on the lumbar region that house all the nerves including the spinal cord. This is a very dangerous region and operating here without explicit consent violates my client's rights. Therefore, the doctor concerned is guilty so as the senior doctor who delegated the tasks. What the junior doctor did reflected the views and stance of the senior doctor. The junior doctor reflected the image of the senior doctor. Having said that, I would conclude that they were all aware, and this was widely practiced and accepted. The senior doctor knew."

"I had no idea and had nothing to do with this."

Diana clicked her fingers, and the usher brought a remote control and gave it to Diana.

"Ladies and gentlemen there is more to this than meet the eye. I present to you exhibit 2 a tape recorded by my client the day he met the senior doctor."

Everyone started talking to each other.

"Objection fruit of the poison tree. The tape was obtained illegally."

"Your honor given the case that they operated without consent and that they tried to cover up everything I think my client was entitled to have this as proof. We are talking here about an institution that is accountable and which owes a duty of care to many people and the public. This is not an individual case where the fruit of the poison tree ground can stand. In the light of the evidence that this was not the first time this has happened I think it's in the public interest to establish that without this kind of information the doctors will keep on abusing the system knowing that nothing will be done. The life of a young boy was abruptly ended, and the father is justified to know the truth."

"Overruled."

"You still owe the hospital money $2000 pay first then we can talk about this. By the way how is your son?"

Was the recorded voice of the senior doctor? The court burst with noises as the people talked about the tape.

"Ladies and gentlemen this was blackmail at its worst. The way she asked about my client's son is an arrogant cunning way, knowing that they were using his son as bait. I can play over and over this tape but the fact will remain that the senior doctor knew what was going on with his son. The time my client insisted on getting the details of the junior doctor, the senior doctor ordered him outside while she made a call. Instantaneously my client's wife phoned saying that at that very moment in time his son had fallen unconscious. The call was in private and after some time he went back in the senior doctor's office. As soon as she had mentioned the money, the next thing she asked was his son. When he first entered the office, there was no mention of his son. She seemed unconcerned about his son. It was only later after he argued that the insurance covered everything and refused to pay that the doctor asked about his son who was in deep pain at that very moment. I conclude that the senior doctor knew and might have ordered this to happen. My client had never met the junior doctor before. All correspondence and meetings were between the senior doctor and my client."

Later that day Richard and Katherine got into their car and drove back to their house. This day was different from all the other days. They were all exhausted. The past weeks they were in and out of the court. It seemed that they were not getting anywhere. There was too much bureaucracy. There was hope at first and now it seemed everyone was involved and the cover-ups just got completed. You could tell they were all lying. I guess it was like one man fighting the entire world. Richard looked at his wife and smiled. She looked back but felt very upset.

"Darling maybe we should just give up. The entire system is corrupt we will never get justice for our son. It seemed everyone is involved. Maybe I think you were right. Do you fancy a cozy night? Maybe try for another baby. I just want to go back to where we were like before."

"We can never be the same again. Our son is dead. My son is dead. Robbed and murdered on my watch yet they pretend that nothing happened. What happened to if you don't fight for this one you will never give me another one?"

"I am exhausted. I am drained. I might suffer a nervous breakdown. I cry myself to sleep. I cry in the bathroom. I miss my boy. Just yesterday I dreamed about him only to wake up to this. Why us? What did we do wrong? Richard my love."

"Nothing. These murderers had gone unchecked for too long. They pretend everything is okay when my son is decaying underground. You were right just fighting in the court is not enough."

"Spend the night with me. I think a new baby will bring a closure to this. If you love me, then do this for me, for us."

Richard looked outside the window as they drove home. They arrived home and after a shower they made love and slept. In the middle of the night Katherine woke up and touched the bed on Proposer's side but he was not there. She staggered to the bathroom. She used the toilet and went out downstairs looking for Richard. She looked through the window and saw the garage light on. She headed back upstairs and into the bedroom. She slept until morning. Five o'clock in the morning when everyone was still sleeping she heard the front door being opened. She heard footsteps into the spare room then into the bathroom and finally the bedroom door was opened.

"Where have you been?"

"In the garage, just couldn't sleep. Looking for me?"

"Not really I woke up at midnight then I saw the garage light on. I just knew it that you might be smoking and needing sometime alone."

"I love you. Everything is going to be okay. Maybe after all this, we find another house in a different city and start again."

"You promise?"

"I promise."

"I love you Richard?"

Richard got on top of his wife and looked at her for a while. She was still stunning as the first time they met. Shining brown eyes and sexy small lips. She had dimples and long blond hair. He remembered the first days they were making love for a baby. That was out of this world. It was so emotional for the two. It was something they had planned, and it felt so right.

"So, what are you waiting for?" Asked Katherine.

As soon as Katherine had said this, Richard slumped on the side of the bed and looked at the ceiling.

"Karl could be with us today. He would be turning nine by the end of this week. It's so emotional for me."

"Everything will be okay just don't do anything stupid. Let's try again for another baby. OK?"

"OK. We better be going the court is starting very soon. I promise after today we should spend more time together. Try for another baby. Thanks for being in my life."

"I love you too."

There were cars everywhere. For most this was like any other day. People going to work to earn a living, for Richard and Katherine this was a big day. A few more days and then the court will be over. This was a long and stressful day than what the couple had anticipated. It was such a traumatic experience. As they near the court a lot of people were gathered alongside the road with banners and cards. This was a big story. It started to emerge that the couple were not the only victims. Others had suffered in silence but hell was about to break loose. This was just the tip of the iceberg. The doctors had become so corrupt exploiting loopholes and taking advantage of the people's pain after the death of a relative to foster a sustained campaign of intimidation and blackmail. Killing and taking whatever they wanted at will leaving a trail of death. A hideous crime. A cat walked outside toward the court yard. A lot of people were going in the court preparing to hear the hearing. The cat walked in between the people until one of the reporters kicked it by mistake causing it to run in the court as well.

"Kitty out. Kitty out. Go, come on, outside now."
Shouted the usher.

The cat ran out of the court and disappeared underneath the cars. Richard wearing a suit without a tie went in hand in hand with Katherine. They sat in their usual position. Richard looked at his watch. He looked at everyone. First at the Judge. Then at the doctor who carried out the operation and then at the senior doctor who delegated to the junior doctor. He looked at the second doctor who referred them to this senior doctor and then to the other consultant and further he looked at the female nurse who was with the junior doctor when they operated on his son. He looked at his watch and at every one of them and smiled. Katherine caught him smiling and elbowed him in his ribs.

"Ouch what are you doing?" Whispered Richard.

"You what are you doing smiling at these murderers?"

"No I wasn't."

"Yes, you were I saw you."

The court was in session and everyone listened attentively.

"What's wrong you look nervous. Stop fidgeting. Will you?" Said Katherine poking Richard in the ribs.

Richard suddenly got up and trembling with anger he tried to address the court. The usher advised him to sit down, but the Judge raised his hand and advised him to continue.

He looked face to face with all the doctors concerned. He looked at the senior doctor.

"All you hypocrites you are sitting here pretending to be innocent when you know exactly what happened to my son. You sit here with all these arrogant faces pretending everything is right when my son is food for the worms as we speak. If I were God, I swear you would all be food for the worms by the end of the day. I guess you are too smart and too connected for anyone to stop you."

Richard touched his ribs and looked at his watch soon he sat down. Katherine heard a beeping noise coming from Prosper's watch. Instantly Richard slumped his head on the table. Instantaneously Silverdale dropped to the ground. The senior doctor hit her head on the table followed by the junior doctor, the nurse and the other doctor. It happened in split seconds by the time the first scream was let out there was blood dripping down on to the flow. All the doctors had a bullet hole in their foreheads. The doors suddenly burst open and the court security guards with guns entered the court room. Everyone panicked some ran out for their life some ducked down. The Judge ducked down as well. Katherine touched her husband and cried uncontrollably. She looked everywhere and saw all her enemies dead too but how come Richard slumped too? Minutes later Katherine drove the car and Richard was in the passenger seat looking lifeless. Katherine drove as fast as she could and headed to the hospital. She looked troubled. The car was near the hospital when Katherine heard a voice.

"Take me to my son."

Looking at Richard she lost control of the car for a while sending the car swerving in front of oncoming traffic.

"Darling you are alive? Damn don't do that again. I thought you were dead. Oh, Richard I had thought that I lost you. Somehow, I felt relived much relieved at least my son's killers are dead too. That felt very good. Were you behind all this? How did you do that? I have never seen anything like this. I will never understand you." Said Katherine.

Richard opened slightly his eyes and smiled. The car drove toward the cemetery out of the city.

Rose-Marie opened the house door from work.

"Darling I am home!"

She shouted leaving her car keys on the table and her coat on the court hanger. There was no reply but the sound of the television was on. She walked into the kitchen and then the lounge area.

"Tim, you are home why you didn't reply me?" She slumped on the couch next to Tim who was listening to the news.

"Very sorry, listen to this."

"What happened?"

"Five people were shot dead today. Three doctors, the defending attorney and the father of the victim to be precise."

"Where and why,"

"In court and in front of the cameras."

"Who will do that?"

"That's what I am trying to find out."

"So, what happened to the shooter?"

"They can't seem to understand how this happened. No one knows who killed them."

"But I thought you said that they were shot in the court in front of the cameras. Someone might have seen the shooter."

"They have shown the footage, but the bullets seemed to come from nowhere."

"That's strange don't you think?"

"That's what I am trying to find out."

Somewhere in the city the door of one of the offices opened, and a man walked in. He looked worried. There was another man sat on the comfy chair.

"Should I not be worried about all this?"

"I think you should but not necessarily."

"Did you see the footage?"

"Several times."

"What do you make of it?"

"I can't tell who is behind this but whoever is behind this is a very dangerous person."

"We are all at risk who knows who might be next?"

"So, who was carried out of the court in the footage?"

Dimitri leaned forward and looked at the footage again.

"That's a good question."

There was silence for a while. The two men looked at each other.
"If he died why carry him in such a hurry?"
"You are right I think he was still alive."
"They might have taken him to the hospital."

CHAPTER SIX

A car parked outside one of the house in the suburban area. Four men got out and entered the yard of the house, two of the men went behind the house. One of them broke into the house through the front door. Minutes later he came out and signaled to the other men and all of them entered the house. After a while the men came out of the house and jumped into their car and drove off. At the same time in the city a car parked outside the hospital and four men got out and entered the hospital. After some time, nearly an hour the men got out of the hospital and entered their car. One of the men by the name of Terence got out and took out his phone and dialed a number.
"He is not here. We checked everywhere."
"Then where is he?"
"Probably dead boss."
"I can't take any chances I want to see his body."
"Copy that."

The car after the call sped off the hospital grounds heading to the city. The wheels of a four-wheel drive nearly ran over a black crow in the road eating the remains of a dead rabbit. The bird flew at the last minute into the air causing the driver to panic and swerve off the road before gaining back his position. The car drove for a while before it passed a cemetery on the left side of the road. The driver looked on as a car was parked further away. The passing driver looked everywhere expecting to see a group of mourners burying their loved one. To his surprise, he did not see anyone. It could be the undertaker's car he thought to himself. The car passed the cemetery. Richard was in the cemetery with Katherine sitting on top of their son's grave. A crow flew from nowhere and landed on the grave in front of the couple. The crow turned away before flying down on the graveyard looking for food.

"Feels like just yesterday when we were a happy family."

Katherine did not say anything instead she looked at Richard while hugging him. Richard turned his head and looked in Katherine's eyes. He lowered his head and kissed her on the forehead.

"At least our son can rest in peace now."

"The pain in my heart has subsided, but I am scared."

"Scared why. We should have a normal life now."

"What if they find out I don't want to lose you too?"

"They can never find out."

"Are you sure?"

"I was shot too, remember?"

"I just want things to go back to the way they were. We can start our family again."

A beep sound cut the conversation between the couple. Richard looked at his watch.

"How can that be?" Questioned Richard

"What is it Darling?"

Richard looked very worried and troubled. He sat up straight.

"What's up? You look like you have seen a ghost."

"Nothing." Replied Richard but Katherine knew there was something wrong serious enough to give her husband that face.

"I think we should not go back to our house for some time."

"You are scaring me now."

Richard hugged Katherine.

"Just to be on the safe side. Nothing to worry about."

One afternoon it was raining in the city. A man in one of the city buildings walked to the window and looked outside. He looked in the road below as a car parked outside. He looked everywhere and noticed that most people were hiding from the rain. Suddenly the car door opened, and a woman got out of the car. and entered the building. She looked nervous and very upset.

She knocked and entered the building. Francis was in the office. A middle-aged man with a sharp chin and broad jaws.

"That bastard tried to kill me. I am sure it's him." Explained Dr. Twinkle

"What do you mean? Please sit down." Said Francis pointing at the chair in front of him.

"It could have been me."

"You mean the day in the court?"

"Yes."

Francis looked down for a while pondering all this.

"So, who was in the court?"

"Maurice."

"The Maurice? Dr. Maurice."

"Yes. Get in touch with whoever is responsible as soon as possible and tell them to say to the media that it was I the one-shot dead."

"Shouldn't you be celebrating that you survived? I understand your enemy is dead too."

"I have a gut feeling that he is not dead. Or he might send someone else's to do the job."

Francis dragged the phone in front of him and dialed a number. Dr. Twinkle got up and walked to the window. She looked outside. It was still raining. She turned around and looked at Francis.

"What's wrong you look like you have seen a ghost?"

Dr. Twinkle walked toward the chair and sat down.

"What if he has marked more than one place? I just don't understand how he did it."

"The general feeling is that he had paid a marksman to assassinate the doctors."

"Including himself? I don't think so." Replied Dr. Twinkle.

"Don't forget this was a man on the edge. The general feeling is that he was suicidal?"

"If you ask myself I think that's all incorrect."

"Incorrect Doctor? I think this was more than a fair statement. The loss of a child in that way is traumatizing." Dr. Twinkle remained silent.

"Don't forget it's not only the loss of a child but it's everything including what he called lies and cover-ups."

"Don't traumatize me as well just get in touch with the right people including the coroner at the hospital."

"Already done."

A white limousine was on the road heading away from the city center. Two men and a woman are in the limo at night time as the limousine headed out of the city center. The atmosphere is that of celebrating. Buzzing voice sounds filled the limo as it cruised toward the city center.

"Tomorrow we are going to achieve a stride in humankind's history." Said the lady in the limo who happened to be the Vice President.

"To the future, for riches and prosperity."

"Tomorrow will be a big day for us a big day for human kind."

"What's happening tomorrow?"

The following day a limousine arrived outside a big building that has been newly built and stopped outside. A red carpet was outside laid down already. The Vice President got out as soon as the usher had opened the door. She looked everywhere and before she knew it she was partly blinded by flashes of cameras. She smiled and looked in every direction. A lot of people had gathered outside. She waved and smiled. She walked on the comfy carpets heading toward the building. She looked in front of her only to be greeted by a lot of people who had gathered. Among them was a familiar face that of the Professor. A well-educated man who represented the future in its glory. A man of substance, one who meant business. Since his years at the university the Professor had a vision. He wanted a world in which he can predict what was happening. He dreamed of a world in which he can predict what people were going to do. His ideas were met with much controversy because to achieve what he was proposing would mean abusing and infringing people's privacy and access to data rights.

"Professor I bet now you are sure that your theories don't work in modern life. To achieve what you are proposing Professor would mean trampling on all these people's rights. We are not talking about privacy rights only, we are talking about access to data, hacking, infringing on human rights you name it."

"Mrs. Vice President where there is a will there is always a way."

"The world is changing what was right yesterday can't be guaranteed to be the same next year. People's values change. I don't want the world to gang up on me, I mean us."

The Professor walked toward the Vice President and breathed out heavily and lowered his head toward the Vice President.

"What if I tell you that I have discovered a way to achieve all that?"

"Professor I am answerable to many people and I am accountable for my actions. There is a lot of weight on my shoulders."

A report came from nowhere and interrupted the Vice President and the Professor.

"Mrs. Vice President with all due respect I don't think the money you are spending here and what you expect to achieve justifies that. This money could be better spent somewhere else."

The Vice President walked toward the reporter and looked at the Professor and everyone. Everyone started gathering toward her.

"I will answer your questions at the end after the ceremony but let me emphasize one thing. The world is changing so as we. We don't want to be in a situation when diseases and crime brought havoc to our people. We want a society where I the Vice President know exactly what you are thinking and a world we can predict with much precision what you will do next."

A reporter interrupted straight away before she continued.

"What about infringing on human rights? Rights to private life. Right to privacy. Rights to less infringement and interference by the government. What about the rights of all these people?"

The Vice President looked down for a while and then at the Vice President.

"We are working on a solution where we will never infringe on privacy and human rights."

"Mr. Vice President I don't mean to sound rude but there can never be what you are proposing without you the leader breaking rules and abusing your own people."

A huge buzzing noise cut through the silence. People started talking. This reporter had a point. The Vice President is the worst person to uphold privacy and human rights yet she expects everyone to abide by the rules.

"Now you see why we need these $billion. I didn't say it will be easy but I am saying that together we can achieve this. Just imagine a society where we know exactly what you are thinking. A society where every time you leave your house we know exactly where you are going. Just imagine a society where we know exactly what you are going to buy every time you enter the shop."

The same reporter interrupted.

"Exactly that's what I am talking about. Somehow you are breaking the law in trying to anticipate all this. You must be infringing on people's privacy somehow."

The Vice President smiled for a while.

"It's you again." She laughed as everyone looked at the reporter.

"Yes. We can do this just by analyzing the information we hold on our database."

"Mrs. Vice President you are not taking us very seriously. We take the invasion of our privacy seriously. We don't care you are the Vice President. You are answerable and accountable to us, the voters."

"Young man I will make you vanish."

"I guess you perform magic as well now." Replied the reporter cunningly.

The Professor looked at the Vice President and nodded his head.

"Mrs. Vice President allow me to demonstrate."

The Professor took out a gadget in his jacket. He took out a small film from the machine and walked toward the reporter. Young man lick this film. The reporter tried to refuse.

"Listen nothing to fear just your saliva and you will see some real magic."

The crowd started cheering.

"Go on Son, it's you who is disputing this. Go on then."

The reporter conceded and licked the film. The Professor placed the film back into the gadget. A moment elapsed as he played with his gadget. After a while the Professor looked at the Vice President who nodded in turn.

The reporter jumped as if scared by something.

"Why you so jumpy?" Asked one of the reporters.

The Professor called the other reporters to see what was on the gadgets.

The machine had predicted that he was going to jump scared which he did.

"Can you scroll down?" Asked one of the reporter.

The next prediction is that he was going to rub his face as if stung by ants. After that the gadget predicted that he was going to jump up and down shaking his pants.

Everyone looked at the Professor and before they knew it. The reporter was screaming and rubbing his face. Followed by him shaking his pants and jumping up and down. The crowd started laughing and cheering.

The reporter looked at the Vice President with worry and fear.

"That's what I call magic. Now you want to disappear?"

The reporter looked at the crowd and then at the Professor before talking to the Vice President.

Later that day the Vice President officially opened the biggest research lab in the country. Billions had been controversially been spent here and every year $billions were proposed to be poured here.

CHAPTER SEVEN

Somewhere in the city a man got of his car and soon after he was flashed by lights. He stopped and covered his eyes with his hands. Moments later a screeching sound of the tires sends him panicking as another car arrived from behind him. He turned around to see what was going on and before he knew it, the car moved toward him in full speed. Quickly he got back into the car and reversed in a direct line with the car. The approaching car did not swerve and the man in the car swerved at the last minute. The car behind clipped his car on the side-front as he swerved out of its way. The driver was Evans, a middle-aged city mega millionaire. He looked scared for his life. He drove quickly heading toward the exit to the car park. He had never been this scared before. He looked backward and saw all the three cars following him. He twisted the steering wheel as he made his way out of the car park. His car exited the car park the front part hitting the road and sending sparks into the air. He lost control for a while as he looked behind him sending his car swerving in front of oncoming traffic. The sound of the horn of the other car caused him to panic even more but soon afterward he gained his posture and drove away from the car park. Three cars followed him and the chase continued. The cars followed overtaking and meandering as they closed the gap. Evans looked ahead of him and saw the slow-moving cars ahead. He panicked and accelerated hard first opening the gap before reducing speed as he approached the slow-moving traffic. A motor bike suddenly appeared next to his car, and the driver wore balaclavas he looked at Evans and suddenly Evans was drawn to the gun mounted on the passenger seat. It seemed the gun was controlled by the handle of the bike as he slowly moved the handles the gun shifted as well aiming at Evans. Quickly Evans reversed his car before seeing his side window smashed into pieces. He bumped into the following car. A screeching of car tires deafened Evans' ears. The driver of the following car conceded and let Evans reverse moving left to right avoiding cars heading forward. Soon he saw the three cars approaching. He placed his leg firmly on the gas pedal and held the steering wheel tight. He knew if he is to hit the cars in reverse his car might not be badly damaged than if he had to bump on them front wise. He tested which one driver would make way for him and reversed as fast and hard as her can. The drivers called him bluffing until he was very close making way for him at the last minute. As he was passing the other cars, he heard a shot on his screen and as he looked backward, he felt his car shaking and a big bang. He hit his head on the steering wheel before an air bag covered his face. He heard a continuous horn sound, and he slowly lifted his head to look in front of him. He saw the cars reversing toward him. He looked in front and saw steam coming out of the bonnet. He felt his head heavy and passed out. He later woke up to see someone on the driver's side door touching his head. He slumped his head onto the air bag before feeling a sharp pain in his neck. Adam was in the city center walking when suddenly he heard a beeping sound. He looked at his phone and a message was displayed on the screen. He stopped and removed his sunglasses. He looked pale all sudden. He was never this scared before. He looked at his watch again. He scrolled and activated the search mode. He took out his phone and dialed a number. He looked nervous as he waited for the other person to answer.

"Come on. Where are you? Pick up the phone now.!" Shouted Adam talking to himself looking at his watch and his surroundings. After a while a female voice answered the phone.

"Listen very carefully. Check on the system I need my exact position. I need the coordinates and search ten meters' radius. Check the recording and play back in the phone. I will synchronize now."

The other person was his girlfriend Christie. She was alarmed by all this. She knew something was going on.

"What is wrong why you sound so nervous and serious?" Asked Christie worried about Adam.

"Check my position now and play back the last five to ten minutes. Hurry I am losing time my system is shutting down."

Christie frantically typed something on the computer and seconds later a beeping sound sends her screaming.

"I got your position and the coordinates. You can start synchronizing now."

Adam quickly scrolled on his watch and synchronized.

"OK ready start the play back."

Silence broke out for a while. Then suddenly the past ten minutes of Adam's journey is replayed.

"Turn up the volume a little." Shouted Adam.

They both could hear Adam's footsteps as he walked in the city center and then a female voice saying greetings to someone. They could hear the cars and the noise of people shouting on the other side. This went for some time before they heard some noise as if Adam collided with someone else. Seconds later they heard Adam apologizing and the man cursing and shouting a single word. Instantly they heard a beeping sound.

"Pause, right there. That's it. That's the culprit. I need the coordinates hurry I am running out of time."

Soon afterward Christie gave the coordinates to Adam who ran as fast as he can to the place where he had collided with the person.

"I found the place try to locate which direction that person has gone."

"Why is that important?"

 Asked Christie out of curiosity.

"Yes, I need the other word to rest my system. Hurry my system is shutting down anytime now. Go back on the system. Search five minutes within this radius at the exact time." Shouted Adam looking at his watch and looking around.

Christie instantly started scrolling on the system and started the play back.

Three minutes into the search they heard a beeping sounding and quickly Christie gathered the coordinates and gave these to Adam. Adam ran in the direction where the person who had collided with him went. He arrived at the position.

He scrolled on his watch and waited. After the beep, he selected ignore last command at these coordinates and reverted the system to a previous state.

"Say the magic word first." A message came from his watch.

"Bullet." Shouted Adam hysterically looking at the minutes left before system shutdown.

"Incorrect magic word."

"What! There must be a mistake!" screamed Adam.

"Please say the magic word again."

Adam cleared his throat before he said the magic word.

"Bullet."

Incorrect magic word system shutdown activated countdown 5 minutes to system shutdown.

Adam looked lost for a while. He played back the recording.

"Christie. Play back the recording. What was the word said by this bastard? I have less than ten minutes hurry my Darling."

"It's bullet! Bullet Adam. Bullet."

Shouted Christie hysterically.

"What!? I thought so too but it's not. I tried it twice. I have one chance left now. Play back again 4 minutes left."

Christie screamed as she rushed to the computer and frantically punched the coordinates. A man's voice can be heard saying bullet before they heard footsteps only. They both repeated the word at the same time. "Bullet!"

"3 minutes before shutdown one last chance left." Christie screamed as she walked up and down Adam's study room.

"I am sure he said bullet."

"That's what I thought too, but the bastard is too clever. Damn. I never suspected this at least now. Oh, Christie I feel like I have been robbed. I have so many things to tell you. I love you."

"Damn! Don't give up we still have two minutes. Let me think. So, you are saying he said bullet, but he did not say bullet. Does this has to be a single word?"

"Yes, one word not a phrase."

"Damn! I was about to say pull-it."

"No Darling that's a phrase. It has to be a word."

"Maybe he meant it that way to disguise the word. OK I have an idea let me check something."

Suddenly Adam sat down. He looked at his watch and saw a minute left displayed on the screen of his watch. He started feeling his chest tightening and having difficulties breathing.

"Christie. Christie." Faintly said Adam calling his girlfriend on the phone.

"Hang in there."

"I will just try the word bullet for the last time. Thirty seconds to go."

Slowly the system started shutting down. He felt weak and weak. He looked at his watch and only ten seconds were left.

He could hear his girlfriend crying replaying back the recording.

"I am sure he said bullet. Please don't go. Don't die on me. I love you Adam. Please hang in there. Just try again."

Adam looked around to see everyone minding their business as if nothing has happened when he was probably breathing his last breath. He smiled and took a picture out of his girlfriend from his wallet. He looked at his watch there were only three seconds left, with a faint voice as he feels all his energies going he tried the word bullet for the last time.

The time he last checked there was only a second left. Fainting lying on the bench he whispered his last word.

"Pullet."

Christie frantically screamed on the other side as a second was left before shutdown. It was very hard and painful for her that she didn't even look. She threw herself on the carpet and started crying hysterically.

Minutes later she heard a voice on the system's speakers.

"Deactivating sleeping mode. Your system has been reset." After a while she heard a beeping sound and a female voice.

"Good afternoon Mr. Adam. How was your short nap? Sorry for any inconveniences caused your system has been reset as you requested."

"Adam! Adam! Adam!"

Shouted Christie on the other end.

"Yes Darling." Replied Adam getting up.

"Oh, you are alive I thought you were dead. Oh, my love I thought I had been robbed too."

Adam smiled and touched himself. He tried breathing very hard, and it seemed everything was normal after all.

"Play back the last minutes. I don't understand why it didn't work in the first place."

Christie smiling jumped onto the computer and played back the last recording.

"It sounds the same, bullet." Shouted Christie.

Adam looked confused and worried for a while.

"OK ask the system to tell you the last magic word."

A moment passed and a beeping sound was heard and Adam quickly looked at his watch. A message was displayed.

"Pullet."

Instantly Christie shouted the same word.

"It was pullet Darling not bullet."

"Damn I almost died today."

"What I don't understand is how your system has been hacked like that. I thought you said only you have the voice synthesis code?"

"I don't know that's something I have to find out."

Adam soon after went straight back to his car. He entered his car and drove heading to the suburbs.

He knew he could have died. Today sheer luck served his life. He realized the dangers of this system. He remembered his father vehemently opposed to this. He used to lecture him about how he was giving his life into someone's hands. At that time, no one believed him until his death. Seventeen years has gone by and the reality has started to unfold. Surely his enemies were about to kill him. Today he survived only because of his father. Although he never believed his father not because it was lies no but because of the fear. He knew everyone was going through this. This was preached to be the new era but his father's fears were being confirmed now. Those who claimed to protect you today are the very same people who are going to kill you tomorrow. As he was driving somehow, he entered that mind frame just seconds before the system nearly shutdown. The sound of the horn from the oncoming traffic woke him up from this state. He opened the CD compartment and took out his best CD by Linking park and played his favorite tune, My December. The car drove up the hill into one of the most expensive areas to live. Over the years his friend Kirsty has immersed a huge fortune as people started coming to her for advice and solutions. Adam parked outside and got out of the car. He stopped and looked at the houses in that area first. This was life at its best. He smiled for a while. He felt like he had been given another chance. He didn't want something like this to happen again to him.

He looked at his watch then at the gate and he saw a camera pointed at him and soon afterward the gates started opening. Adam jumped into his car and drove in. Later Adam is talking to this beautiful lady, late twenties with a beautiful smile. She had long painted nails. She looked at Adam and smiled.

"Adamsky what brings you here. My dear old friend."

"Just want to enjoy your life style as much as I can life is too short you know."

"Don't scare me. People who talk like this in my experience they have experienced a near death experience. So, want to come out in the open. What really is your problem, Adamsky?"

"OK you are right. They nearly killed me."

"Hacked your system?"

"Not just that they changed the voice recognition system as well. This bastard today said just two magic words, and I was a goner within minutes."

"You have problems with those in power?"

"Not that I know of. What makes you say that?"

"They are the only ones to kill that way. They have got the money and the resources to do so." Replied Kirsty.

"What? I don't understand why me?"

"You will be surprised this is a highly sophisticated grooming and money laundering scheme so complicated that no one knows that they are like cattle being reared at a farm or some poultry for that matter ready to be killed and sold as meat."

"Really. Don't scare me like that."

"You said it yourself that you nearly died."

"It sounds much worse with the way you are saying it."

"Look at it as a business. There are people who they call cash cows, the dogs, the stars and the question marks. The cash cows are people who cost them a little they don't spend time monitoring you or your investments they know they can count on you. So, in other words you cost them little but you bring a lot of cash for them, either stealing it from you or after they have murdered you. There are also the people they call the stars. These people generate a lot of money but they must spend a lot of time and effort guiding these to make money so that they can milk them after. These are the people who have their own businesses but who depend on them for customers and everyday needs. Then there are people called the dogs. With these people, you spend little on them and you get a little out as well. These are people they don't worry or care about because what you invest is what you get back. The last group is that of people called the question marks. With these people, there are more emotional factors considered arriving at decisions. Relationships with these people are purely emotional rather than financial. They consume a lot of their cash but generally generate very low incomes."

"What kind of people are these?" Asked Adam curious.

"These people normally fall in the category of blackmailers and other people which they have ties with. They take a lot of their time and cash but bring little or no money back and these are a very majority of the people they have."

"So, you are saying they rely heavily on the cash cows for a cash-flow influx?" Asked Adam.

"Exactly. These people have the self-drive. They don't rely on them for anything. So, they spend less on them but milk a lot from them. These are the people like you. This is mainly the target group. All these dirty tricks are witnessed by this group than any other group."

"So how can they tell I am a cash cow or not?"

"Don't forget this is a multi-billion-dollar project. They have analysts who work all day and all night just profiling you. For example, the common characteristics of cash cows are that they are laid back after they have accumulated a fortune they won't care much. They like the outdoors. They like green color. They are easy to milk. They don't complain you can hit them repeatedly they don't complain. Have you ever been given a parking ticket, and another and another before you knew it you have loads to pay? In the end, you don't question why so you end up paying for many within a brief period?"

"Yeah but I never thought that's important."

"You probably have a lot of green or you are attracted to green. To them all these are indicators that you are a cash cow and can be easily milked,"

"I think it's just coincidental?"

"They look at people who you associate with. Look at people who they call the question marks for instance. These people never associate themselves with anything green. They like red or brown colors. They fight for every penny they have. They can't be milked instead they spend more money and time on these than say the cash cows."

"I never thought about it that way."

"Green advertise you that people can easily rob you. They can easily abuse you. They can hit you with ticket after ticket and you will still pay. You make more and lose a lot too."

"How can we survive in this world?"

"Opt out, for most they were forced or didn't even know they were into this scheme until they started having these issues. Everyone is included even without their consent. Talking about human rights abuse. Breaking of privacy laws. I swear there is going to be a war soon. One of these coming years they will mess up with the wrong person."

 Kirsty walked to her computer and started typing something on the screen.

"So, you had a near miss?"

"I could have died today. How did that happen? Even now I still don't know."

Kirsty looked at the screen she entered Adam's serial number into the system. A warning light started flashing on the screen.

"Damn. You are in great danger. You are programmed to have died this afternoon. Hey what's happening."

Kirsty sat down and quickly typed something on the keyboard.

"How did you do that? I think you are the first one to have dissolved not just two booby traps but also in the shortest time. Wait, a minute."

CHAPTER EIGHT

Kirsty looked at Adam first before opening another screen.

"This has never been done before. How did you guess the magic words? The odds of you guessing the words within ten minutes are infinity to one it's unachievable. You have beaten their system. Damn even myself I don't think I can dissolve one booby trap within such a brief period, Adam. Damn you are good, man. Did you just guess both magic words?"

Kirsty looked at Adam worried and surprised.

"Damn I thought I was the best hacker in town but you Adamsky boy today you surprised me. Honestly how did you do that?"

Adam at that very moment realized that maybe he had played a part after all in saving his own life. He had attributed all this to luck.

"I continued on my father's plans after he died. His idea was that at any given time a person can be in two places which can then be synchronized into one and time can be delayed and then the two be linked together."

"Oh, My God! All these years I never thought about it. Your father was a genius Adamsky."

"I only knew after he died and ever since I have applied his ideas and today I should say he saved my life."

There was a moment of silence.

"OK let's see your system now maybe it has reset again and updated now." Said Kirsty playing with the keyboard.

"What did you do? Why these people are after you that much?"

Adam moved close to the screen and looked at Kirsty.

"What makes you say that?"

"You won't believe this you have three more booby traps that will require a magic word all within ten minutes over a large area otherwise you are dead meat."

"Dead meat? I thought this was over?"

"I bet they noticed you have offset the traps and now they are making it harder for you."

"Why can't they just get the money and leave me alone?"

"You know too much after all it will be daylight robbery. When you are dead eh who cares?"

Adam sat down and touched his head.

"Can you disable the booby traps?" asked Adam dead worried.

"Nope! If we go through what you did first, we can devise a plan. They have a count down so we can be prepared as we know what time exactly they can go off."

Kirsty and Adam worked all night on a plan to try to diffuse the booby traps and anticipate when they will try to deactivate his system. It's the ringing sound of Adam's phone that did sends both panicking.

"Hello Darling. Where are you? Please come home now. I am scared to death. Please come home."

"Sorry Darling I can't there is more to it than I can explain right now. You know what if I give you an address will you drive up here bring your night dress we sleep here?"

"Are you with a female friend?" Asked Christie feeling jealous.

"That's not important are you coming or not."

"No, it's important you listen to me. I stayed with you all these years and today you nearly died guess what? The first person you run to is that woman. What about me? I waited for you all day. No calls or anything. Maybe you make me think twice about all this."

"I love you!" Shouted Adam.

"You upset me all the time. Why not run to me first? I don't like to be second best you know that. She better not be your girlfriend or ex-girlfriend."

"You talk too much you could be on your way here by now."

"OK I love you see you soon. My Adamsky."

"Who was that?" Asked Kirsty feeling jealous too.

"That was my girlfriend. Christie, oh she is a lovely lady bit nervous all the time but a really good lady."

"Why you didn't tell me that you have a girlfriend?" Adam looked a little confused.

"Are you serious? I guess you didn't ask. Is that important? I thought men like me are out of your radar. You are one of the richest ladies I know men should be throwing themselves at you."
Kirsty touched her hair and looked in the small mirror on the table.
"They just want my money for most I can't have a conversation at the same level as I do with you. I had a crush on you at high school."
"Yeah. Yeah. Just because Antwan is not around. What happened to me and my Antwan?"
"I said I had a crush on you even though I was in love with Antwan."
"That's good to know now that I am about to be milked and killed or should I say killed first and then milked."
"I just thought you should know before you die." Said Kirsty smiling sarcastically at Adam.
"Yeah very funny." Replied Adam looking annoyed.
"OK on a serious note do you trust your girlfriend?"
Adam stood up and walked toward the window in the room before replying Kirsty.
"What kind of question is that she is my girlfriend of course I trust her?"
"You are not being honest with me Adamsky. Do you trust her?"
Adam posed for a while.
"If you trusted her why you came here alone? Why you didn't tell her you are with me?"
"Listen she is a very jealous and possessive person. I didn't want you to see us fighting."
"How did you meet?"
"Listen Kirsty my life is on the line and you waste time about my girlfriend."

"Listen you will be putting me into danger too. I have to believe I can trust her before bringing her in here."
"OK I see what you mean."
"Listen Adamsky I am not trying to be funny you know. See why I am alone? Because I don't trust anyone. I don't want to be a cash cow not yet you know."
"I know what you mean."
"OK give me details as soon as possible. I ask you a question reply straight away don't think. Close your eyes. OK. I will try to build a profile of your girlfriend."
 Adam laid on the couch with his eyes closed. Kirsty opened another screen after a while she looked at Adam.
"Are you ready?"
Adam cleared his throat and replied.
"OK. What is the name of your girlfriend?"
"Christie."
"What is her favorite color?"
"Blue,"
"What color are her eyes?"
"I repeat what color are her eyes?
"Blue."
Kirsty paused for a while and went through the other screen.
"Why are we stopping have you finished already?"
Kirsty did not reply for a while she was murmuring something.
"You took a long time to answer. I said no thinking don't make me repeat the questions okay. We try again."
"What is your favorite color?"
"Green- blue."

"If you are to choose one what would it be?"
Adam did not reply straight away.
"I guess blue."
"OK I will ask you another question. At home, how many green shirts and t-shirts you have estimate?"
"Seven."
"How many blue shirts and t-shirts you have?"
"Three ah four."
"Have you ever got angry at your girlfriend?"
"Not really?"
"Have you ever hit her."
"Never."
After a while Kirsty stopped talking and concentrated on compiling the report. The report was nearly complete about to be displayed on the computer laptop when a knock on the door sends both taking cover.
"Damn that's a strong knock. She scared us that must be your girlfriend."
Adam removed the scarf he had put around his eyes and went to open the door. As soon as Adam had opened the door Kirsty heard a clapping-like sound.
Christie entered the room first followed by Adam who was holding his chin.
"Who are you? Can you believe this I nearly died thinking that he has been killed and guess who he run to the very first time he woke up from dead? You. Don't even ask. You deserved that." Said Christie looking at Adam.
Kirsty raised her eyebrows.
"Hi, I am Kirsty Adamsky's best friend."
Christie looked worried.
"She even calls you Adamsky I thought it was only me. Kirsty what do you want with my boyfriend?"

Christie looked around and realized that she must be very rich. Quickly she went to Adam and hugged him soothing his cheek she had set on fire.

"I am sorry babe. You know you nearly died today. You should have come to me first okay. I am not made at you. I am just saying that you should be with me you know."

Adam kissed her on the forehead.

"I am with you babe. Okay."

Christie looked at Kirsty and spoke to her.

"See he is not after your money. He loves me."

Kirsty looked annoyed by the way she treated him.

"And you do you love him. Please! Give me a break. I am not stupid you know. You are just advertising him to the highest bidder. Who do you work for?"

"I can slap you too you know. I can kick your ass right now if you try to disrespect me in front of my man."

"Ladies see, why I was keeping you two apart. I don't have time can you fight after I am gone?"

"Where are you going babe? This time I will go with you. Don't leave me okay."

Christie hugged Adam for a long time and tears ran down her cheeks.

"I can't breathe." Said Adam realizing Christy's tight grip.

"Are they still setting up the booby traps? I don't understand but I love you. All this should have stopped by now."

Kirsty looked at Adam who looked at her in return before they all looked at Christie.

"Who are you talking about? Do you know something about this?"

Kirsty quickly flipped the laptop before closing it. She looked at Adam with a strange look. Adam remembered the last time he saw that look. He knew what it meant. The three of them went through the plan together before Kirsty took Adam and Christie to the guest room before herself going upstairs to sleep. Fear struck Adam. He knew the look on Kirsty's face. He went to sleep. Just after midnight Christie was fast asleep. Upstairs Kirsty was wide awake. She was busy pondering what could have been if Christie hadn't turned up. This could have been a steamy night for them. They normally say people have more passion after a near death experience. She heard footsteps in the lounge room downstairs and quickly got up. In her night silk badge dress that clung to her body revealing every perfect shape God gave her. The more her silk dress caressed her nipples the quicker she made the steps going downstairs. On the other hand, Adam was a bit suspicious about his girlfriend. Surely Kirsty must have discovered something. He remembered the time she nearly had a fight with Christie earlier on surely, she wanted to use something in the laptop probably that profiling report. Adam limped forward to the laptop. He took a long breath and opened the laptop. He switched it from sleep mode.

He looked at the screen and cursed. Kirsty's voice startled him.

"It's shocking to know, isn't it?"

"You made this up. Did you?"

"The truth hurts, she is just a cash-cow parader. Oh, she loves me oh she loves me. She will get you killed. Probably she is the one behind all this. I bet she work for them right now."

"Are you telling me that this computer thinks I am 80% more likely to have been marked as a cash cow than not?"

"The figures don't lie. You nearly died. If you die today who will benefit the most?"

"Probably her. Funny I was thinking of adding her to my will."

"Wrong she works on commission at most 5% of what your value is."

"Even if she is on my will?"

"Commission only clause."

Christie woke up and looked next to her. Adam was not there. Jealous and anger choked her. She got up as soon as she heard voices. She staggered toward the lounge room.

Just in her undies she wrestled with Kirsty

"What are you doing? Are you fucking my boyfriend? Are you? Tell me right now."

The two women fell on the couch one on top of the other. Christie gripped Kirsty's hair, and the women scratched each other. Adam looked for a while before hustling to separate the women.

"I don't want her in my house. Get out right now!" Shouted Kirsty her bloused torn with her twins hanging out. She didn't even bother to cover herself.

"I told you he is mine stay away!" Replied Christie dragging Adam to their guest room.

CHAPTER NINE

A black SUV parked outside one of the city buildings. There were security guards everywhere. This seemed like a government owned building. The man in the car wearing a baseball cap sat in the car looking around everywhere. The man in the car looked at his watch as another car approached the building entrance. The man in the black SUV got out and walked toward the other car. After a while he walked back to his car and waited. As soon as the other man had come out of the building. The man in the SUV entered the building and signed on the reception desk and headed upstairs. He entered a big conference room and quickly opened his bag. He took out his gear and measured the area. He took out his laptop and keyed in some coordinates. After some time, he packed his gear and was about to leave when the door opened. He did not expect anyone as it was late at night. A short man entered the building wearing an overall carrying window cleaning equipment.

"Who are you?"

"You who are you?"

"Obvious I am the window cleaner?"

"Why they sent you they told me I am working here tonight?"

"You really. I have worked here for more than 3 months now."

"There must be some mistake OK I will go and find out."

The man from the SUV took his bag and walked downstairs looking backward as he leaves. He was about to enter the lift when he saw the lift indicator showing that someone was coming upstairs. Quickly he took the stairs and went down as fast as he can.

There was a security guard siting on the desk.

"Sign out" Shouted the security guard.

"OK just a minute I am just taking something from the car for the window cleaner."

The man from the SUV jumped into his car and sped off. The security guard heard the screeching of car tires outside and he got up and went to look outside. The window cleaner's car was parked outside and there was someone in the car, he could see a shadow of the head. He went back inside and went upstairs. He looked around everywhere and when everything was okay, he went back downstairs.

Days later, one night Gregor the window cleaner had a fight with his girlfriend. Upset he jumped into his car and headed for work. It was the same old job for him. He has been doing this for as far as he can remember. He loved this job. This was easy money for him as he would like to put it. Tonight, was like any other night get in get stuck in and the job is done in no time. The security guard on the desk heard the screeching of car tires before seeing Gregor open the door carrying his gear.

"Who are you visiting?" Asked the security guard looking at Gregor.

"What? It's me Gregor the window cleaner."

"Yes, but where is your uniform? You know the rules."

Gregor looked at himself and cursed. For the first time, he had just entered the building without his trade mark overalls.

"Oh sorry." Replied Gregor going back to his car. Minutes later he returned but without his bag with the tools. He arrived at the reception and looked around.

"Lost something?" Asked the security guard after noticing that Gregor was looking for something.

"I thought I left my tools here. Unless."

He didn't even finish his sentence before going back to his car. The security guard looked at him and shook his head. Gregor came back a few minutes later and went straight upstairs. The guard sat down minding his business when suddenly, he heard what sounded like a gun shot. He panicked and unclipped his gun and ran upstairs. He was about to open the door when the doors opened hitting him sending him falling onto the stairs. Gregor went through the door as fast as he can. The guard got up and advanced forward. He peeped into the room but the room was empty. He looked around but there was no one. The room was empty all the windows were okay. He checked all the other rooms before going downstairs. He looked around for Gregor but he had already gone. His car was no longer outside. One sunny day a limousine parked outside the building. A large crowd had gathered outside people holding posters and banners were outside while others were cheering and welcoming the Senator. The Senator was a tough woman she had campaigned to pass a bill upholding data protection and privacy rules among other environmental and pollution bills. She had been praised by some and despised by many. To the business community she was an obstacle to development. All the bills she proposed only slowed or cost the businesses more money. Nevertheless, some loved her especially the old and retired members of the population who made up most of the well-wishers as she arrived for the conference meeting. Her bodyguards got out of the limousine and looked around first before she followed suit. She looked around and waved. This was the best part for her. These pictures in most of the time would make the tomorrows headlines. Wearing hired clothes and jewelry she was envied by all. She was also a fashion icon. The tabloids loved her. They knew she sold papers. That could explain why there were so many tabloids people around the time she arrived. Cameras slashed from every corner nearly blinded her. She took her time walking slowly on the red carpet. She was more than a celebrate. She knew how to tune everyone into falling in love with her. She stood at the entrance to the building and looked back at the reporters. She raised her arm and waved. The bodyguards looked at each other before one of them looked at her. She knew she had taken too long but hey, she didn't care she was in the driving seat. She entered the building, and she stood in front preparing to give the speech when suddenly, she looked pale and frightened. The body guard after sensing changes in her body functions went to her.

"What seemed to be the problem Mrs. Senator?"
The Senator looked around for a while. She looked lost. She looked at the bodyguard.
"Nothing just my wild imagination."
"No madam. I sensed changes in your body activities. What are you afraid of? Tell me so that I can make the correct decision. Is it safe for you? Shall we go back?"
The Senator looked around. The smiles of all the people and the limelight gave her courage otherwise she might have canceled the meeting.
"I sensed fear. If you don't tell me how can I help you. You know protocol Mrs. Senator."
The Senator looked around and moved closer to the bodyguard and whispered in his ear.
The bodyguard looked shocked and held her hand about to drag her off the stage of the conference room.
"No, no, no. Go and check first tighten security make sure no one comes in. One of you should be at the door. This meeting has to go on."
The bodyguard stood there for a while before talking to the other bodyguard. After a while everyone started cheering and clapping hands as the Senator took center stage. The bodyguards checked everywhere and made sure that there was no one suspicious.
"Ladies and gentlemen, I am working very hard making sure that your demands are passed as law bills in parliament. I am going to lobby until all your interest are passed into bills. Tonight, we are going to look at pollution and environmental bills that I have already lobbied. There are amendments that are

required. Talk to your representatives and get back to me before the next meeting."

There was a buzzing sound as everyone started talking to each other. Some clapped hands and cheered on the Senator. As everyone was busy talking to each other a few people screamed. The bodyguards looked at the Senator. They rushed to her. She was down holding her handkerchief in her hand. She looked around and saw the bodyguard. Mark the bodyguard looked at her. Her dress was covered in blood. Soon the blood patch seemed to be growing. He frantically pressed down the wounded area to stop the bleeding. He looked at her and apologized.

"Call for help now!!" Screamed Mark.

Looking at the Senator.

"Hang in there. Hang in there. Help is on the way. Oh, my God! I should have listened to you."

Moments later a lot of people had gathered around. No one heard anything they only saw her down. The other bodyguard Chris looked around with a gun in his hand. Mark spoke on the radio and took out a florescent light and projected what seemed to be the bullet trajectory path. Chris looked at the projected path and moved toward that area. As Chris was busy searching for the shooter Mark was busy attending to the Senator. Possible major artery damaged. The bleeding was uncontrollable and soon she was drifting into unconsciousness. By the time help arrived she had already died. Mark got up and helped Chris look around for the killer. The two men frantically looked everywhere for any signs of the killer. They searched the adjacent rooms and even ran outside but there could not find anyone.

The President entered his office. He heard a knock on the door before he replied the Chief National Security Officer entered the office marching like a soldier with his cap in his hand.

"It's with great sadness Mr. President. The Senator has been assassinated."

"What? Who will touch government officials?"

The Chief National Security Officer walked to the table and grabbed a remote control for the television and switched it on.

"Just in. In a bizarre occurrence, the Senator was shot dead in front of everyone but no one seemed to have seen the shooter. It is understood that her bodyguards were present and now left traumatized by this ordeal. The President has been informed and her close relatives. It seemed the country is on alert after 4 doctors had been slaughtered in similar circumstances just a few weeks ago. Eunice reporting for Touch ladybird lucky news."

The President walked to the window and looked outside for a while.

"Who is doing this?"

The Chief of National Security did not reply he looked confused himself.

"Can you set up a task force to look at this? I want whoever is behind this dead."

Weeks later the place was cordoned off as the officers investigated the killing. The special squad looked around the whole building looking for clues. Gregor had been taken by the special squad. In one of the buildings in the city Gregor woke up to find himself in a small room with big window glasses around it. In the middle was a desk with a chair. The big door opened. A man dressed in a black suit came in.

Gregor felt relaxed he had feared that it could be a member of the special squad. His lawyer maybe he thought. He raised his hand and sighed.

"Who killed the Senator?" Asked the man as he sat down.

"I don't know to be honest."

"Why did you run away who do you work for?"

"I work for myself. Somebody tried to kill me so I ran away."

"Who tried to kill you?"

"I guess the other cleaner the last time I saw him he was not very happy to find me there."

"There is another cleaner? What does he look like?"

"Big man. Hey look. I had no time to look at him. I went to do my job. I saw him there I told him this was my job. So, he left."

"The guard said you ran away acting strange probably drunk one night and never went back there again is that correct."

"Drunk me? No. I fought with Julie. I went there okay I wasn't myself. I was upset so what. I got in I started cleaning and douche-bag fired a shot at me. I ducked and ran as fast as I can. I never went back there again. Die for that me no. Fuck the job I got my Julie we are happy."

"Who shoot at you?"

"Douche-bag who else. I just heard a gun shoot and ran."

"Do you own a gun?"

"No."

Days later an old lady called Rose entered the building pushing a trolley. She was humming a song as she proceeded to the lifts. She pressed the lift button and waited. A bell rung and soon after the lift door opened. A man wearing a cap and overalls got out of the lifts and stopped as the women's trolley was blocking his way.

"Madam." He said looking at the old lady.

"Sorry Sir."

She replied moving her trolley out of the way. She looked at the man as he walked through the door. He was carrying plastic bags, and he was wearing blue gloves. She entered the lift and was taken upstairs. On the top level, she entered the conference room. This was the first time she had been here since the assassination of the Senator. She took out her gear and started cleaning the place. After some minutes, she sat down and ate her cake. Minutes later the placed was very clean she looked around and walked to the back of the room. She went to the left window and looked outside. It was beautiful outside. It felt strange for her as she always cleaned the place very early in the morning. It was now afternoon. The building was to be reopened soon. She walked back to her trolley that's when a bullet casing fell in front of her. She looked upwards and everywhere. She looked confused. She knelt and picked up the bullet casing before screaming and throwing the casing back on the carpet. She looked at her hand and saw the imprint of the casing. She wore her glove and picked up the casing. She looked at it and later left it on her trolley and left the building. Days later Rose entered the lift with her trolley as usual as the doors were about to close fingers protruded holding the lift doors. The doors opened and Rose looked at the man. She realized that she had seen this man before. The man when he saw that there was not enough space in the lift because of the old woman's trolleys he stood outside and decided to wait for the next one.

"There is room for all of us. Please come in." Said Rose pushing her trolley to one side. The man entered the lift helping the old woman push her trolley to one side. In the process the bullet casing dropped. The man looked on the lift floor after hearing a sound of something falling but couldn't see anything. The lift stopped, and the woman pushed her trolley out and left the lift she waved bye and left. Detective Jesse remained in the lift. In his head, he was trying to find out how the Senator was assassinated. The President was pressing for answers and the head of the killer. The noise of the lift bell woke him up from a trance he was in. The doors opened and a beautiful lady waited for the lift. Detective Jesse looked at her before going out of the lift. The lift closed behind him as he walked away. Soon he was on his way. A few seconds later he heard someone calling him.

"Excuse me! Excuse me. Can you wait for a second? I think you dropped this?"

As soon as the lady had given the detective, the bullet casing she walked back to the lifts area. The detective looked at the casing and tried to piece everything together. Soon afterward he ran to the lifts. The lifts were way up he decided to take the stairs. He went up the starts and when he was about to open the door the door suddenly opened wide hitting his hand sending the bullet casing flying down to the ground. A man in a baseball cap had instantly opened the door wide hitting the detectives hand with the door making the detective Jesse lose the bullet. The bullet casing can be heard hitting the ground floor. The two men looked at each other. Detective Jesse was way up the stairs and it was a long way down. The man with the baseball cap was going down, anyway. For a while the two men looked at each other without saying anything.

"That's mine keep that safe I will be down in a minute, will you? I need to see someone first." Said Detective Jesse.

The man in the baseball cap looked down first before replying.

"I am going down anywhere I will leave it with the security guard at the desk."

Detective Jesse excited that could be the breakthrough he wanted looked for the old cleaning lady. Instantly as he opened the door, he saw her going into the conference room. He ran toward her.

"Excuse me Mrs.!"

The old lady stopped and looked at the detective. The detective arrived breathing heavily.

"Take your breath my son, I am not going anywhere." Said the old lady.

"In the lift, you dropped a bullet casing where did you find it. Which room. Please show me where."

Pleaded the detective.

The old lady did not reply but instead looked at her trolley.

"I am sure it was here. I left it here." Said the old woman looking on her trolley.

"Yes. I have the casing but where did you find it?" Questioned the detective.

The woman signaled to the detective to follow her. She pushed her trolley into the conference room. The detective heart started beating very fast with every move she made. She left the trolley and walked to the back of the conference room and looked around before looking into the air. Once she looked up in the air, she raised her hand up. The detective moved close to her. He looked around.

"Are you sure." Asked the detective.

"Yes of course. It fell on me I was standing here."

"What? Fell on you. I thought you found it on the floor." Asked the detective perplexed.

"No, it fell from the ceiling. Look what it did to me."

The detective looked at the women's burnt fingers and acted as if he had seen a ghost. He sighed in disbelief.

"Are you sure the bullet casing did that to you?" Asked the detective looking at the old lady's fingers.

"So, the casing was still hot" Said the detective talking to himself.

"What?" Asked the old lady.

"It's okay I was just thinking out loud."

The detective looked around.

"Okay remain in this position okay." Said the detective running toward the front of the conference room. He arrived where the Senator was standing and took out a trajectory light and reflected toward the old lady.

"Damn. That's the one."

The detective walked toward the old lady.

"When did you find the bullet casing?"

"A few days ago, in fact the day before they reopened this place."

The detective looked in front of the conference room thinking.

"Still it doesn't make any sense."

"What does make any sense. I told you before outside about all this." Said the old lady feeling annoyed.

"We spoke outside?" Asked the detective not paying any attention.

The old lady cursed and started walking toward her trolley.

"I am just old I am not stupid you know. I remember talking to you outside but you were wearing a cap that time."

The detective looked surprised.

"You mean today."

"Yes of course."

"Damn!" The detective ran outside and straight toward the stairs. He ran as fast as he can downstairs jumping some stairs steps until he reached the ground level. He scanned the ground floor first and cursed. He entered the lobby and straight to the reception desk.

"The bullet casing! Where is it? The bullet casing."

The security guard at the reception looked lost.

"Did someone leave a bullet casing with you? A man wearing a baseball cap?"

"No. I don't think so. He just went straight out."

"Damn! Son of a beast!"

The detective ran outside and looked everywhere but there was no one. He ran back inside he looked at the visitor's book on the desk and went through all the names. He went back inside and looked at the ground floor level for the bullet.

He kicked the door very hard and cursed.

"I nearly got him. That's the killer. Bastard."

The door opened soon after.

"Are you okay I heard some noises?"

"Detective Jesse."

He flashed his badge.

"I nearly got him. That bastard has some nerves coming back here."
He breathed very hard and walked around before radioing the headquarters.
"I need extra eyes twenty-four seven conference building over."

CHAPTER TEN

The screeching of car tires sound caught everyone's attention. The woman at the reception looked outside in the car park. She saw a man got out of the car and walked very fast toward the entrance. The man was detective Jesse. Early thirties with a tie and cross-belts. He pushed his hair backward as he entered the building. He stood in the reception area and searched his pockets. He walked out of the building and straight to his car. He looked at the dashboard and took his electric cigar. He puffed out a lot of smoke that seemed like a small cloud as he walked back inside. He entered the building and looked at the receptionist.

"She is waiting for you."

Said the receptionist looking at detective Jesse.

The detective arrived outside the office of the Sergeant. He puffed his cigar and as soon as he had puffed out the smoke the door opened and the Sergeant looked at him.

"We talked about smoking that thing in here, you are not different to all these guys you know."

"It's electrical."

"So, it is still smoking indoors."

"Not in this state."

"You better have some good news the President just phone me. He wants answers he promised extra funding if we can get this killer."

The detective stood up and walked to the window. He looked outside and breathed heavily before coming back and sat down.

"I met the killer today. I am sure it's him."

"Is he dead now?" Asked the Sergeant.

"Dead no. He escaped."

"He escaped? Why you didn't shoot him. Dead or alive we don't care."

"It happened so fast. I had the bullet casing in my hand?"

"I thought in the report it is said that no casings were found on the scene?"

"You won't believe this the casing fell exactly two weeks after the day of the incident."

"Fell from where. I am not following?"

The detective got up his face shinning with excitement and explained what happened.

"I think I know now a little about this killer. He is a very educated and sophisticated person. We are playing with a real pro. He ain't no ordinary crook. Somehow, he knew the casing would drop today after the crime scene had been cleared. That means he is very much aware of our methods. So, if it happens again now I know when to go and wait for him."

"Are you out of your mind? Wait for him? No What if he targeted the President or the Vice President for that matter? I want him dead right now. I can't take any risks?"

"I promised you we will get him. He made a mistake, or I was just lucky. I now know what he looks like."

"Go to the artist department I need a sketch right now. Whatever he is using is too sophisticated that we can't just stick around. Find him!"

 A car left the car park in the city and headed to the posh suburbs. The driver was Dr. Twinkle she had spent the entire day with Francis after the shooting. This ordeal had traumatized her. She knew that it could have been her if it wasn't for her genius plan. For the first-time in her life she had trusted her instincts, and this had paid off. She survived the assassination plot. She felt guilty too as she had tricked her friend into going. The only thing that was worrying her was the fact that if the killer find out that he had killed the wrong person and that she was still alive he might come for her. Moments later a man stood in front of her car but instead of slamming on the brakes she swerved the car and in doing so nearly collided with another car causing herself to bang her head on the door. She looked down and saw blood droplets on her legs. She looked in the rear-view mirror and saw her face. She had a scar on the forehead that was bleeding. Afraid that it could have been the killer she didn't stop. She drove off looking constantly in the rear-view mirror. She parked the car in her driveway and rushed inside quickly opening the door and leaving the keys on the door. She smudged her blood on the door and walls inside the house. She dropped on the floor and wriggled kicking the stand nearby. The candle that was on that stand fell. She crawled upstairs coloring the carpet with blood. She pushed the bedroom door with her bloodied hand and fell on the floor. She bumped her head on the wardrobe very hard causing her nose to break. She started bleeding. She wriggled on the floor and ripped the arms of her dress and removed one of her shoes. She got up and opened her hand bag. She took out a small plastic container and shook the contents. She dropped droplets on the floor and smudged the heel of one of her shoes on the floor. She touched some contents and touched the curtains and the walls. She went back downstairs dropping blood droplets here and there. She went back into the car and took the pair of shoes in her car and smudged these on the ground before wearing them. She imprints the prints next and near hers all the way upstairs and back before removing the shoes and getting into the car she drove off and called the police.

"911 what is your emergency?"

"Someone is trying to kill me. Please help."

"Can you see this person right now.?"

"Yes. He is following me. He is in the car behind me. He tried to kill me at my place. Please help."

"Where are you now we will send help?"

"I don't know. Eh somewhere along Gilchrist road. Please help."

Dr. Twinkle stopped the car and reversed into a parked car and drove off miles away she stopped the car and threw away the shoes and continued with her journey.

Minutes later she saw a lot of flashing blue and red lights and stopped the car. She remained in the car until the officer arrived. Among them was detective Jesse. Dr. Twinkle was bleeding and bruised all over.

The police cars went back the way they came hunting for this killer.

"So, where is he?" Asked detective Jesse.

"I don't know but he was following behind me. He tried to kill." She sobbed uncontrollably.

"OK come with me I will take you home we need to take a statement."

Detective Jesse drove home with Dr. Twinkle. The other police cars followed them while the other car left cordoning the place.

Wait in the car this is a crime scene now I will find somewhere for you to stay first we need a statement. The other police officers marked the place and cordoned off the entire house.

The car drove to the police station.

Later the doctor and the detective are talking.

"Do you know this person?"

"No I don't know him."

"Tell us what happened."

The doctor looked scared and confused. She sobbed for a while before talking to the detective.

"I arrived late from work. As soon as I arrived another car parked just behind me. I thought he might be visiting the neighbors."

She paused and wiped tears from her eyes.

"I looked at the man but he was now talking on the phone. I parked the car and got off. I looked at the man again now a little suspicious but the man remained talking on the phone outside his car. As soon as I inserted the key in the door and opened the door but without retracting the key. I heard what seemed to be footsteps. When I looked back, I felt this sharp pain on my forehead. He was holding something in his hand that he used to hit me with. I staggered inside and fell to the ground. He tried to sit on me but I wriggled very hard and kicked him. I crawled upstairs, but he soon followed. We struggled again upstairs."

She paused and sobbed.

"He nearly killed me you know. I knew if I don't fight him he was going to murder me. In the bedroom, he pulled me very hard tearing the arms of my dress. Instincts kicked in I just removed one of my shoes and hit him in the face very hard. He covered his face with both hands I ran downstairs and into the car. After that that's when I called you. I had left my purse in the car."

The detective listened very attentively taking notes.

"You are in safe hands now. Do you know why he might have attacked you? It seemed he might have followed you home."

"Honestly I don't know just find and arrest this monster kill him if you have to."

She covered her face and sobbed. Days later she was staying in a hotel with full surveillance. The detective collected samples and evidence and left. After the investigators collected samples Dr. Twinkle was allowed back to her home. One raining day a car parked in the car park of the research lab in the city and detective Jesse got out of the car and ran inside covering his head with his waist coat.

"Damn! I can't believe it's raining. It has been raining all day. Good for you stuck in here the entire day."

"Detective. Glad, you came we were expecting you."

"You must have something good for me."

Innocent smiled and looked at the detective before getting a report from his desk.

"The rest of the reports are in the office."

The detective browsed through the pages and read the bottom part.

"Are you sure this is correct?"

"The manager will explain everything."

The detective walked out of the lab and into the corridor and knocked at the door of one of the office. It was minutes later when a female voice replied.

"Just a minute."

A man came out of the office wearing a suit and with a report in his hand. The manager stood outside the door.

"Come in Detective."

The detective stood waiting to be told to sit. As soon as the manager had finished filing the reports, she asked the detective to sit down soon after she sat down too.

"I now have most of the reports concerning this case. The results are disturbing?"

She handed the detective one of the reports. He looked at it and looked at the lab manager with raised eyebrows.

"I don't get it. How on earth would a dead man try to kill this woman?"

"I can't say for sure myself but something is wrong. DNA matched that of the deceased but if he was already dead, then how can he be in two places at the same time. In the grave and at this house?"

"Did you get a report from the coroner?"

"Yes, he died shot in the neck pronounced dead at the hospital."

After getting the results from the lab manager the detective left the lab with many questions. He sat in his car for a while. He read the whole report and drove to the doctor's house. He parked his car outside feeling a little upset. He knocked on the door very strong. Minutes later the door was opened. Dr. Twinkle stood at the door.

"Yes. How can I help you Detective?"

Detective Jesse opened his eyes and looked at the doctor with eyes that said don't waste my time.

"I see you seemed very upset does that mean you didn't find him."

The detectives looked around for a while.

"Doctor don't waste police time. If you wanted to know for sure if he was still alive why didn't you hire a private investigator. We can't afford to waste time and the taxpayer's money you know."

The doctor looked down and touched her forehead and started sobbing.

"That bastard tried to kill me and now you don't even believe me."

She sobbed uncontrollably. For a while the detective looked confused. She sounded very convincing.

"We have a match but the person is dead. He was shot dead in the court. I saw his death certificate and autopsy report. He is dead. Dead like a dog. So, stop wasting my time."

The detective was angry now. He paced left and right pushing his hair backward.

"Now tell me why you are lying to an officer."

A man came down from upstairs wearing boxer shorts and a big gown.

"Don't yell at my girlfriend. What kind of police man are you? I will talk to your boss right now."

"You piss of shit get out of my face you are wasting my time. You want to talk to my boss. Here is the phone use mine call her now. I suggest you put your tail between your legs and go back upstairs I haven't finished talking to the doctor. OK?"

Detective Jesse looked at the doctor and pushed his hair backward.

"Is this an insurance scam or what? Doctor."

The doctor sat down on the couch. The detective followed suit.

"Detective you said in the report you read that he was shot dead, yes?"

"Yes, in cold blood in the court."

"Who else was shot that day? Can you check the report again?"

"I believe a Dr. Chad and a Dr. Twinkle was shot dead among other doctors."

"I am Dr. Twinkle."

"But you told me you are Dr. Maurice."

The doctor looked outside the window holding her tears.

"We switched. I was the one who was supposed to be in there but instead Dr. Maurice took my place and got shot."

"So, you are Dr. Twinkle presumed dead but you are still here? So, who faked your death certificate and the autopsy report? Wait a minute are you saying that the killer faked his own death and all the reports just like you did?"

"Exactly, he is still out there."

"Blood, DNA?"

"Complicated."

"See why I think you need a private investigator rather than a policeman. This takes time and money and surely you can't afford that."

"How much just between you and me. I want him dead."

After this meeting with detective Jesse the doctor's confidence started coming back. She started going out on her own and doing her regular activities like jogging and attending the gym. There was always someone to watch for her. Whenever the detective was off work, he would spend some time keeping an eye on her at the same time searching for this killer. Richard was sat down typing some figures on his keyboard when his mother-in-law came in. She threw a newspaper in front of him. He looked at it and stopped instantly what he was doing. He picked up the paper and opened the paper. His picture was on the front page. Instantly his wife shouted for him to ran inside. He got up quickly and entered the lounge area. The anchorwoman was on the news.

"A few days ago, a woman was violently attacked in her home and she narrowly escaped unharmed with moderate bruising to her forehead and face. The man pushed her inside her home but fortunately she fought back injuring the killer in the face. She escaped and drove away but the killer chased after her. It was later that the killer disappeared after the woman phoned for help. Members of the public are advised to be vigilant and not to approach this man but to call for help. An e-fit of the man has been released. If you see this man call for help now."

Richard looked at his wife for a while pondering all this.

"I don't get it."

His wife switched to another channel and on another channel, was the latest report.

"DNA analysis from the crime scene has been used to identify the attempted killer as one Richard Jones. Police believe he is still alive, and he is also wanted for the murders of the doctors and the Senator. If you know his whereabouts please dial this number, do not approach him. Lucy reporting for Touchladybird lucky news."

Richard got really agitated. He walked in the house thinking about what to do.

"Darling I don't understand but we pronounced you as dead how on earth can a dead man still be killing all these people." Asked Katherine confused and worried.

"Let me think. DNA. What DNA? It could be a copycat attempted killing?"

"What if someone is trying to frame you?"

"Who? I don't miss. All the people on the to-do-list are gone, done, and buried. Who is this doctor Maurice?"

"Are you sure? Maybe you must check with the hospital? Make sure anyone on the to-do-list is done."

Richard breathed heavily and went into the basement. Moments later Katherine heard the motorbike speeding away. Richard entered the hospital and scanned the foyer first before walking to the desk. There was a female receptionist wearing reading glasses. She saw Richard all covered up wearing shades.

"How can I help you?"

"I am here to see Dr. Maurice."

The receptionist looked on her computer screen and scrolled down. She opened another screen and another screen and another screen. Richard suspected that something was wrong. He apologized and walked out of the building. Quickly he disappeared. Miles away the pager of detective Jesse went off while he was on a motor way. He was heading in the opposite direction in which he was wanted. He cursed and stepped on the gas pedal. He tried contacting Dr. Twinkle, but she was not picking up the phone. He drove as fast as he can and left the motor way using the next exit. The doctor after the gym went upstairs and into the lift. She entered the parking space upstairs. She felt a bit nervous. She looked around and opened the car door. Instantly the door of the car nearby opened, and a man walked straight to her swiftly and pulled a gun without saying anything he pulled the trigger. The bullet noise made the doctor so frightened that she felt like she peed herself. She touched her chest and closed her eyes. The man put his hand in his jacket pocket and took out a watch. He threw the watch on the floor and spoke to her.

"Dr. Twinkle you have been served with a death notice and you have been critically shot and you die in seven days."

The man looked at her and entered his car and drove off. The screeching of car tires sends her into a panic. Somehow, she thought that she was already dead. She opened her eyes and touched herself. She looked underneath for blood but she was still standing. She just couldn't believe it. She knelt and picked up the watch. She looked at the watch. The screen was flashing. She looked at the screen. There was a message that read;

"Dr. Twinkle you have been served with a death notice and you have been critically shot and you die in seven days unless…"

She felt sad. She had heard the same message from the man but she thought that she was dreaming or something.

"Unless what?" She shouted in the car park. Quickly she drove her car out of the car park and dialed the detective's cell phone.

Frantically she tried to call the detective and drive at the same time. Fear ran through her spine. It was moments later that the detective answered the call.

"Jesse here. How can I be of any help?"

"Detective it's me."

"Dr. Twinkle?"

"Yes. Listen I have been shot. This guy shot me."

"Are you bleeding? Go straight to the hospital we meet there."

"No. No. Come to my house. He said I die after seven days."

The detective looked confused. He jumped into the car and drove to Dr. Twinkle's house.

CHAPTER ELEVEN

On arrival, he saw a car parked outside with the driver door open. He jumped outside quickly and pulled his gun out. He approached the house and found out that the door was open. He entered inside and saw the doctor lying on the couch touching her chest crying. He sat next to her and touched her shoulders. She rose and hugged him and sobbed like a baby.

"The bastard shot me today at point blank. It still hurts I feel like my chest exploded. I still can smell the gun powder."

 The detective thought that she was lying. She had no wounds whatsoever.

"What do you want this time? I don't really get you. You don't look like you have been shot. You seem alright. I think he has missed again."

"He shot me he said he never misses. He said I die in seven days. He gave me this watch." The doctor took out a watch and looked at it before giving it to the detective. The detective looked at it and saw a message displayed. He read the message and looked at the doctor.

"Tell me what really happened."

"I finished my gym session and was about to enter into my car when he approached me. He pulled a gun and shoot me then told me that I die after seven days unless."

"Unless what?"

"I don't know."

Dr. Twinkle sobbed for a while and looked at the detective.

"Look, soon after he left this dropped from nowhere."

She took out a bullet casing and gave it to the detective. The detective looked at it and took out a plastic bag from his pocket and placed the casing inside.

"Why would he say unless, if he had shot you?"

While they were talking, the watch beeped. A message was displayed on the screen.

"To unlock this and live there are 5 things you must do. First you must officially admit that you murdered my son. That you experimented on my son before butchering him. Second you must confess that you let Dr. Maurice get killed instead of you. Third you must confess that you planted DNA evidence and tried to set me up but the truth is that I am dead. After you have done this, you will need 3 magic words and the exact locations they were said to unlock this and avoid death. You have got seven days left, bye."

"This crazy son of a beast. You see now why I wanted him dead?" Shouted the doctor tears running down her cheeks pacing left and right in the lounge.

"What magic words and where?"

The detective sat down not knowing what to do. He held his head in his arms for a while.

"So, what do you want to do first?"

"As if I have an option."

"I guess the confessions are easy you would say you were under duress. The scary part is the magic words."

"I am dying anywhere he will never leave me alone. You should see the way he shot me. He did not even blink. I felt the bullet in my heart."

"I saw the bullet casing so I believe you. Where do we start? We need to get the confessions out of the way. That will leave us with plenty of time to crack on with the magic words, shall we?"

Richard arrived at his in-law's home in his black SUV with tinted windows. He sat in the driver's seat for a while. He looked at the picture of his son on the dashboard and breathed heavily. Moments later he removed the plastic cover on the seat and went into the garage. He left his stuff there and entered the house through the garage door and entered the guest section of the house. He opened the bathroom door and came face to face with his wife who had just finished taking a bath.

"What did you do?"

She looked at Richard who was covered in blood.

"Now you are asking me what I have done. You heard the woman she said I tried to kill her but you know me babe I never miss so I blasted her away at point blank."

"Darling, that's a lot of blood."

"You should have seen how my son bleed to death. How our son bleed to death. So, don't talk to me about blood this blood that."

"You are becoming more like them now. In the end, someone else will start feeling like you. When will this end?"

"You listen to me very carefully. I let it go years ago but you call me name you accuse me of not caring. You said I should do something about this. So?"

"I am just saying you are out of control."

"Wait and see after I have finished with them."

Richard took off his bloodied clothes and entered the laundry room and turned on the washing machine. He returned butt naked and looked at his wife who was doing her hair. He jumped in the shower room. He started singing Oh ladybird by Elinadeivid. Katherine wiped the steam off the mirror and paused for a while. In the sink basin below droplets of tears danced to Richard's song. The higher his voice the faster the droplets dance their way in the basin before disappearing in the sink-holes.

I touched ladybird, and I got luck

Oh, ladybird bring me love bring me luck

I have seen your face a thousand times

Every time I blink I see you.

I remember your stole my heart

You gave me wings when you said we belonged

I don't want to hang on to nothing

Bring me love Oh ladybird bring me luck

The moment Richard sang the above verse Katherine sobbed and threw away her make-up kit and wiped her tears. She removed her bathrobe. She walked toward the shower glass door naked and slid the door open. Richard was covered in soap washing his hair when Katherine entered the shower room and started snogging him. The two locked in each other's arms as the song continued in the background coming from

Katherine's mum's lounge area. Later that night Richard and Katherine were talking in their bedroom.

"I have to go for a while. You will be safe if you stay with your parents."

"I want to go with you. I am not a little girl you know."

"I know. If we go together, then you die too."

"Richard don't talk like that. You sound like you are going to commit suicide."

"This woman blew my cover now you understand why I blasted her away. Will be a miracle if I survive this. All the murders. No chance. I might as well cross out the whole to-do-list one by one."

"So, what are you planning to do?"

"You know what I have to do?"

"No. I don't."

"Clean the entire system so no parent will never go through like we did."

"Darling you are not serious. That's fighting the whole country."

"That's why I am saying stay with your parents."

"They are looking for me now. Soon they will come here. If I am not here, you will be safe. Take them to my grave. You will live but I will come for you when this is over."

"I thought you wanted to try again."

"Yes, before all this."

"You should not have killed her. You should at least have asked her to confess that she was just setting you up but you are dead."

"Yes, I told her. that."

"After you shot her.? What help is that to us?"

"She is still alive she has seven days left."

"Have you heard yourself? Richard try to make sense. You are confusing me now. Then whose blood was it you came covered in?"

"Darling let's just say it's complicated. One day I will explain this to you. Most of this right now, is also new to me."

The following morning Katherine woke up to find that Richard had left her parent's house. A limousine cruised in the city heading to the newly built building in the city. Inside was the Vice President. She was on the phone talking to the President.

"Mrs. Vice President stay safe there is a lunatic killing government people. You should always travel with bodyguards."

"I know Mr. President. I am just going to see my research lab I have some business to take care of."

"I have set up a task force to hunt this killer. You never know tomorrow he might target me or you for that matter."

"Put up a reward. He will be dead in no time. I will see if we can help as well."

The phone conversation continued for some time before the limousine arrived outside the newly built research lab owned by the Vice President. The newly recruited Professors, technician and lab assistants were all waiting for her outside. A huge applause was given to her as she got off the limousine. She smiled at everyone before the Professor approached.

"Mrs. Vice President. Welcome. We are honored to have you today."

"The pleasure is mine Professor."

"Shall we?"

The Vice President and the Professor entered the building followed by the rest of the people. The Vice

President was shown different sections and achievements since the lab was opened. Later the Professor and the Vice President went into the Professor's office and started talking.

"We have a problem and the President wants to know if we can be of any help?"

"Oh! Regarding the killer?"

"Yes Professor."

"I must admit he is a way out of our league. I can't pin him down. I tried but I am not saying we can't get him. It takes time we can locate him but for a very brief time when his system is changing."

"In layman's terms."

"He has built a robust way of escaping so advanced that it's easy for him to kill anyone he likes."

"Did you have a look at the death of the Senator? What can we learn from this?"

"It seemed he has mastered the delayed time mechanism to his advantage. This has enabled him to go undetected. In the case of the Senator. The reports suggested that she knew she was going to be shot, or she had some insight into the whole thing. I understand minutes before she was shot she told her bodyguard that she heard a gunshot minutes before actually getting shot."

"Is it avoidable?"

"I would like to think so. Had she not attended then I think she would have survived."

"How can we get him? I want him alive. We can use him. Find everything you know about him. I want to know everything. Why can't we give him a serial number?"

"He has developed a sophisticated system that place him in more than two distinct positions at the same time. You see. Our system can only work based on a specific location at any given time so we can pin and lock the position and the coordinates of the subjects. With this guy, he moves every time we can't get an exact location to give the serial number and pin him down. We will end up with ghost subjects. But what I can do is to set up booby traps that he can trigger and in the end, we will see his daily pattern movement. There is at least one place he will visit more frequent at specific times. When that happens, he will be our man."

"That's exactly what I want Professor."

"Back to our plan. Since we opened we have managed to chip most of our subjects unknowingly. I think we need another special team. There is still a lot of work to be done. Once that's done we can move to phase two."

"What's phase two."

"The profiling and categorization of all subjects into four groups. The cash cows, the stars, the dogs and the question marks. Once we know who is who we will set up a program that is linked to their bank accounts. Say once they have a certain amount in their bank account we automatically receive a message to start the milking process. In the end, we will be collecting money from everyone systematically. The initial cost is high but once we have chipped everyone and given everyone on earth a serial number. You will be the richest person on earth. We will know everyone's activities through the serial number."

"OK Professor I will leave this to you we will see with time. I will see if I can raise more money for this project."

The Vice President left the research lab. One sunny day the President was in his office. He stood up and walked toward the window. He smoked his cigar and walked back to his table. He pressed a button on the telecoms system.

"Get me the Vice President I want to see her in my office." Said the President.

Later that day a sharp knock was heard on the door. The President walked toward the door and opened the door himself.

"Mrs. Vice President I was expecting you."

"What is the urgency? Is everything okay?"

"I don't know I think if we are the leaders at least we should try to anticipate in advance what our country will experience in the future isn't it so?"

"I guess you are right Mr. President."

The President walked toward the window and opened the small window. He puffed his cigar before putting it off. He apologized for smoking.

"What is going on? Is this the end of the world or what? Are you sure it's just one person doing all this? What does he want?"

"He is just causing panic and fear making people lose trust in you."

The President switched on the television and watched the news. In the news, the anchorman was reporting the phenomenon that has spread all over the country.

"A new wave has hit most cities in recent times. A man has been known to claim to have shot dead hundreds of people asking them to guess the magic word as a way to avoid death. What is clear is that all the people who had complained are government officials? Why he is targeting government official, no one knows for sure. All these people had complained that they have been shot at point blank but without suffering any wounds. The men then go on to give them a watch like this one telling them to go to certain locations and guess the magic words. So far none of the people managed to guess the magic words resulting in instant death on the spot. I am here with an expert who will try to answer some questions. Professor Culrinks why are these people not dying the day they were shot?"

"I believe the killer is manipulating the delayed time mechanism. In this case, he shot's you today but delay that in time by somehow manipulating geographical space-time position in time."

"Professor Culrinks how is that possible we understand it has been proved in animals are you suggesting that these humans have been somehow chipped."

"That's the only plausible explanation. To be able to manipulate the delayed mechanism the system must assign a serial number to you first to be able to identify you and shift you in space-time continuum. This has worked successfully in animals and objects but never witnessed this in humans."

"Please join us again after the main news. Richard reporting for Touchladybird lucky news."

The President lowered the volume and breathed very heavily. He walked to the small window and looked outside. After a while he looked at the Vice President.

"Mrs. Vice President what I don't understand is why government officials. The Senator, the doctors, the attorney you name it. This serial number business, do you have anything to do with this? Do I have a serial number.?"

The Vice President smiled and got up. She walked toward the window as well and looked outside.

"Don't be absurd Mr. President you don't have a serial number. All this talk that they are targeting the government officials is purely coincidental."

"What do you know about this killer?"

The Vice President walked back to her chair and poured herself water to drink.

"The man they are calling the killer was killed, shot dead in the court. What I think is happening is that other copycats are now carrying out the crime blaming the deceased."

"What was his grievance with the doctors?"

"He said they butchered his son."

"So, he was killing all these people just to revenge the death of his son? Was he mad? Can't he make another one."

"His main argument was the way he died. He claimed they deliberately murdered him therefore he is doing the same."

"So, when is this going to end? What has the Senator have to do with this?"

The President sat down and poured some wine for himself.

"He claimed it is a government cover up. To clean the system is to clean the whole government. The Senator passed bills through parliament covering up all this giving immunity to what he called murderers."

"So, does that include me and you?"

"I guess so. Who knows for sure?"

"Listen I can donate money into your program as a reward for his capture. I want him dead. I can't have the whole country worried just because one man lost his son. How many people lose their kids every day?

What is so special about this man? Send my boys to his grave dug him up. I want to see his bones. If he is alive get him. I am the President. I can't let a lunatic terrorize my people like that. OK?"

"OK Mr. President."

A few weeks back the building of the Chief of National Security was surrounded by protesters and members of the public. A car parked outside as demonstrators raised banners and placards. A heavily built man wearing a very expensive suit entered the building surrounded by his bodyguards. After the security checks, he was allowed into the building. He touched his heart as if in pain. He walked and entered one of the office room. Inside were a single big table and chairs around it. A man was sitting down on the other side. Other people all who looked like government officials or executives in suits and expensive dresses were all sat on the other side. The man was Fabian a rich government official. The bodyguards approached as well with him but the man who was seated raised his hand. The bodyguards stayed backward. Fabian sat down in front of the man. The man raised his head and looked at Fabian in the face.

"Hello, I am detective Jesse. Are you a victim also?"

"Victim only. That bastard murdered me in cold blood and robbed me of my dignity."

Fabian clutched his fists and shook his body as he spoke to the detective.

"Where were you shot? You seem fine to me." Asked the detective.

"Listen that bastard approached me I was just getting out of my car. He just looked at me and pulled a gun and shot me in the heart. I feel the pain right now. I still could hear the gunshot sound. I just don't understand how he did it but he blasted me like a dog. I am one of the most powerful people in this city you know? And now look at me I exchange seats with junkies and muggers."

"Did you imagine being shot or what because as far as I can see you are okay? If you were shot, you could be dead you know."

Said detective Jesse trying to understand the man.

"You think this is funny? Look where is the Senator? I bet she came here and told you the same. I bet you laughed at her too."

"No. I am just trying to understand you. If someone shot you in the heart, you will die straight away. You see where I am coming from?"

"This son of a beast gave me this watch he said I should tell him the magic word if I want to live."

"What magic word?"

Questioned detective Jesse curious.

"Why are you asking me? I came here I thought you know. You must be the one who pissed him off."

"But I am not a magician. How should I know?"

"Maybe I am just wasting my time with you."

Fabian got up and instantly his bodyguards got up as well. The detective pleaded with him to seat down. In the city park a lot of people have gathered demonstrating that the government is doing nothing to kill the killer but some protesting that they are the ones who started all this. A buzzing sound thunders in the surrounding building. People were clapping hands some singing and the others waving banners and placards. An armored hammer arrived followed by other cars. The President and the Vice President got out and walked onto the stage surrounded by their bodyguards. Silence broke out. The President and the Vice President threw each other a quick glance before the President took center stage.

"I want everyone to know that we are doing our best to make sure we bring this killer to justice. We are working very hard to make sure that you are safe. That we will operate and carrying out our day-to-day tasks without fear. Like I said we will kill this culprit. We have set up a task force to tackle this issue. Thank you over to the Vice President."

One of the reporters walked toward the stage.

"Mr. President I have a question. They are rumors that the person presumed to be doing this is already dead. What do you have to say about this?"

The President looked at the Vice President and walked back onto the center stage.

"In that case, we are now chasing after his ghost because my people are still dying."

Everyone started laughing.

"Mr. President some would argue that he is actually doing you a favor as he is removing all the rotten-corrupt people in your cabinet."

"I take that as an insult. Corrupt or not corrupt no one should die like that. That's the worse suffering you can ever see. These men and women sacrificed a lot to work for you. They might be corrupt but hell no they don't deserve to die like that."

Replied the President.

"Is it not irony? Bearing in mind that that's the way they killed his son too."

"I can't answer about what happened to his son nevertheless these are my people I will defend them at any cost. Now over to the Vice President."

The crowd clapped hands for the Vice President as she approached the center stage.

"Ladies and gentlemen our country is under attack. No matter how corrupt we are we cannot expect to die such a death. I had a dream, and I anticipated this might happen one day. I have opened the biggest research lab in the world to tackle issues like this killer. I can help all of you but this cost money. I have a developed a way of identifying and assigning serial numbers to all of you so that it will be easy to protect all of you in the future."

A buzz of sound exploded deafening everyone. People talked to each other in groups.

"Mrs. Vice President. This will be going too far. What about our rights to privacy and freedom?"

"I will not stand here and see anyone of you get killed by this killer or whoever is doing this. I will protect you all even if it means infringing your rights. Every one of you will have their DNA taken and a unique serial number will be assigned to each one of you."

"Mrs. Vice President. We have national insurance numbers is that not enough?"

"The serial number I am talking about is linked to you and your geolocation in the space-time continuum. We will be able to track all your movements in case you are in danger. We will be able to shift you in time to avoid death. We will be able to know the magic words. I have concrete information that the magic word is linked to a moment in time and specific geographical location. Without this serial number, it's impossible to do that. This is not optional. This is compulsory."

"Mrs. Vice President I don't think you have the right to tell us what we should do or not do. We have rights to choose."

The President moved toward the center.

"I used my Presidential powers to pass this bill. When a government is under threat as we are, with the Senator and others already dead I can impose a blanket bill for a certain time that will help us deal with the threat and in such that is exactly what I did. As from today everyone will be required to visit the new research lab and leave your DNA so that a serial number can be assigned to each one of you. Any questions?"

"No! You can't do that!" Shouted some people in the crowd.

The Vice President and the President looked at each other before they disappeared.

CHAPTER TWELVE

One evening the limousine was heading out of the city with the Vice President exhausted and tired. All she wanted to do was to go home and take a long bath before going to bed. For the past weeks, she has been busy. While in the limo her cell phone rung.

"Mrs. Vice President, it's very urgent I have located the killer. He is near your office in the city can I send our boys?" Shouted the Professor with much enthusiasm.

The Vice President looked worried and excited too at the same time.

"Professor anything you can do to protect me I would like to meet him?"

"Very risky don't take any chances. I can't guarantee any protection. I have the boys ready to play with him. He will soon disappear. It took me months to track him down. I suggest I send the boys."

"I will take my chances."

"No Mrs. Vice President don't!"

Shouted the Professor.
"Quickly turn around and head back to my office."
Instructed the Vice President to her driver. The car tires of the limo screeched as it turned in the middle of the road and headed back to the city offices.
"I will tell you when you are near him but stay far away from him. Okay?"
Said the Professor.
"I have an idea Professor keep the line live. Okay."
The limousine drove for some time before it cornered into the road where her offices where. It reduced the speed and stopped. A man carrying a bag in a suit but wearing a baseball cap approached from the other side of the road. The Vice President opened the passenger back door of the limo and waited. The man stopped as well and looked around. He was about to pass the limo when the Vice President got out and called the man.
"I am the Vice President you are safe come in let's have a chat."
The man stood in the middle of the road and pulled a gun. He walked toward the limo and entered the limousine.
"Drive! Tell your driver to drive we can't park here not safe for me." Ordered the man.
"You heard the man driver lets go."
The limousine cruised out of the city.
"What do you want?"
Questioned the Vice President.
"Me. Who said I want anything?"
"So why did you come to me?"
"I have heard a lot about you I just wanted to see you before I kill you. How come you finished early today?"

The Vice President froze for a while. For sure she felt tired and left her offices earlier. A sharp feeling of fear ran down her spine.

"Don't be scared."

"I am sorry about your son."

"I don't know what you are talking about."

"Why kill the Senator and all these people."

"They make laws to make murders like you go free."

"I am not a murderer."

"You just don't know it."

"So, what do you gain what's in for you?"

"Nothing I died the day my son died. I am just making sure no other parent goes through this again."

"People die that's life. Kids die too. But the world goes on."

"If it's natural yes. No problem but the work of man. It hurts. No man has a right to take another man's life let alone a kid knowingly for that matter. This was not a mistake they deliberately experimented on my son until he died. What kind of human being will do that?"

Richard looked down for a while and then his eyes met the Vice President's.

"Okay stop the limo I have to go right now."

"What makes you think I will let you go. You have killed many. There is a huge reward for your head I might as well get that reward myself."

"In hell, they don't use money."

"What?"

Quizzed the Vice President.

"Don't make me repeat myself. Stop the car."

"Or else what?"

"It's not me I am worried about. It's you."

"It's me? Why?"

"It's not easy to find the magic word I don't want to see you die Mrs. Vice President."

"Stop the limo now." Shouted the Vice President.

"Tell your men to back off. Anything that happens to me you are gone instantly."

Richard got out of the limo in the middle of the road and walked a few steps before walking back to the limousine.

"Oh. You will need this as well. What is the magic word?"

Richard threw a watch through the limousine window and disappeared into the bushes.

"Shit what have I done? I should have listened to the Professor."

The limousine cruised for a while.

"Professor were you listening? Did he shoot me? He gave me a watch. What is the magic word? Professor are you still there. Professor?"

The Vice President sounded desperate trying to reach to the Professor. In the lab, not far away from the city the Professor had his head in his hands not knowing what to say. It was like a dream for him. He just couldn't believe it. Was this really happening he kept asking himself?

"This is an order I want you in the city center near central avenue. Hurry the killer is on the run." Shouted the Professor.

"Copy that waiting for the Vice President's executive order. Over."

Replied one of the man on the radio.

"God, Damn it! I am giving you an order. Execute my command. This is a matter of life and death. The killer is on the run as we speak. Go now!"

"Roger that!" Replied the person on the radio.

Three SUVs suddenly screeched to a halt on the side road and men with guns got out and entered the nearby woods with search lights. It was getting dark but more was at stake to worry about that. The Professor had summoned his boys after the incident. He seemed traumatized and for the first time he sensed fear and panic in the voice of the Vice President. For the first time, he sent out the boys without the Vice President's permission. She had made a mistake, and he was the only one to correct that. Time was running out. The killer was still on the radar and it was up to him to try to stop this. As far as he knew no one who claimed to have been shot by this killer ever survived.

"Listen up! Take no prisoner. Shoot to kill. Better if he dies first. I repeat shoot to kill. Armed and deadly take caution."

"Copy that!" They all replied in one voice.

The leader of the group gave directions, and the group dispersed covering the area the killer was last known to have gone. The chase begun. After a while Richard took out a gadget from his jacket pocket and stopped. He scanned the entire area and realized that he had company. He scrolled down his watch and synchronized with the gadget. He knelt and turned 360 degrees. He knelt again and turned another 360 degrees. He entered some coordinates in the gadget and synchronized with his watch once again. He calculated some minutes and set the timer every 30 minutes. He carried on walking. Every 30 minutes the watch would beep. He would stop and adjust coordinates and geographical position. After nearly half an hour of traveling he got scratched on the shoulder by a bullet. The chase begun. Richard ran as fast as he can. He was surprised that the Vice President had sent men after him. He regretted not taking her serious. Anywhere he had more problems to worry about than these men.

As he was running, he adjusted his watch. Soon he was out of the woodland and he crossed the road into the nearby suburbs. He kept looking back. He looked for a car. He entered one yard and broke the side window of the car parked there. He opened the door and entered inside. He looked for the key but there was no key. A bullet smashed the windscreen, and he ducked inside. He looked around using the rear-view mirror. He opened the passenger door before kicking it and running behind the house. He jumped the fence onto the other yard. Bullets flew above him as he ducked on the ground. A vicious dog nearly ripped off his thigh. He jumped over the fence only to find one of the man waiting there with a gun in his hand. On the ground and cornered he looked at his watch and then at the man. A beeping sound from his watch put the man into action as he swiftly pointed the gun at Richard who in turn flipped sideways before shooting at the man. Two bullet sounds rocketed the skies. Richard stood there for a split second examining himself. He was okay, but the man was on the ground choking on his blood. Footsteps thumping the ground put Richard in the reactive mood. Instincts kicked in and instantly he jumped over the face and ran for his life. Minutes later he touched his side stomach and fell to the ground. He looked at his watch a flashing message was now being displayed after a beeping sound. He quickly scrolled and adjusted the coordinates and soon the bleeding stopped. He got up and staggered away. He ran as fast as he can and quickly he was on the other side of the suburban area and about to cross the road when an SUV suddenly stopped in the middle of the road. He instantly ducked. Two men got out of the car. He looked over and saw that the driver was still in the car. Quickly he looked at his watch and scrolled down punching some figures in. That took a few minutes, but it seemed like ages. A beeping sound went off. It seemed the driver heard this beep sound as well as he reacted and looked in the direction where Richard was. He flicked the headlight switch from dipped lights to full beam and looked in front of him. Richard ducked quickly even more. Another beeping sound went off and a flashing message was displayed on the screen He looked at the watch and saw a message;

"Identified serial number in the vicinity is 000111… Confirm synchronization now."

Richard quickly confirmed and looked at the driver. He heard footsteps from the other side where the two men had gone. He looked at his watch again. A new message was now on the screen.

"Please enter the coordinates for the movement in the space-time continuum."

Quickly Richard entered the coordinates and as soon as another beeping sound went off Richard aimed the gun at the driver. He waited a few seconds to get the right shoot and a few seconds before the others returned carrying the other injured man the driver heard a gunshot noise. He ducked within seconds the window screen was smashed. The other men ducked as well. Richard got up and ran for his life. The other men carried the injured man into the car and the men shouted to the driver to driver. For seconds the driver looked lost. He did not react. The window screen was broken into pieces.

"What's wrong? Have you been shot? What happened?"

Quizzed one of the men.

"He is getting away drive!"

The driver acted like he had been in a trance. Suddenly he started the car and drove forward jerking the car as he goes forward.

"Stop the car!"

Shouted one of the man before getting off.

He ran after the killer on foot.

The driver later regain himself and drove after Richard.

"What happened there? Why you reacted like you did?"

"I don't know I felt like he blasted my face. I had this feeling that I was in a dream of some sort. I just couldn't move. I don't understand what happened to the window screen. It went down first before I had the chance to duck."

"What are you saying man?"

"He shot me."

"No, he did not. You could be dead by now like Braven."

"But Braven never miss especially considering that he might have been shot at close range. How come he is still running? He should be dead too."

"That's what I thought. Braven might have missed. He might have surprised him."

"Where are the other's?"

"Covering ground ahead of us trying to pin him down."

Zephyr had chased after Richard on foot. He was very close to shooting him down when instantly Richard ducked first before instantaneously and swiftly flipped in the air three times landing on three separate places before instantly firing back nearly catching Zephyr off guard. From that moment, Zephyr knew the killer was more experienced than him. No one could have anticipated that. That was Richard's trade mark kill shot. Richard ran for a while before he turned around instantly and fired first with lightning speeds nearly taking Zephyr out. Fence after fence the two men played chase. To kill this killer, Zephyr grasped that he had to play a mind game. He realized that all along he was playing Richard's game. It was time to up the game. He comprehended that Richard followed a pattern of some sort. He ran and after a while instantaneously attacked out of the blue. He knew somehow, he was tired and probably injured as well. He adopted a new strategy. The best he can do is to attack constantly then drop back. He checked his gun and pulled another one from his socks. He advanced. As soon as he had seen the killer he fired continuously with two guns before dropping and ducking. Richard later fire a shot while Zephyr was already ducked onto the ground. That frustrated him and he stopped and looked around. Zephyr smiled and aimed and a split second before he fired the voice on the radio sends him taking cover.

"Don't shoot him. The Vice President want him alive. I repeat do not shoot."

"Damn! Lucky son of a beast! He could be sitting on the table with Jesus right now."

Shouted Zephyr.

"Over subject tired and probably wounded 30*NW and 25* SE. Need back up."

Sleepless nights fatigue and anxiety caught up with Dr. Twinkle. The past two days were the very stressful days she had had in her entire life. It was a countdown to death. The killer had given her just seven days to reset the system or perish. As far as he was concerned he had finished his job. She was top on his so called to-do-list and it seemed he had already done her. Probably already crossed out her name off the list. If she had the luck to see the list probably her name was on the top of the list. As the story goes, he conceded that he had done her already and buried her. It was weeks after the first massacre that he realized that somehow, she was not among the first victims despite dominating the top position. He later found out that she had made smart moves and let her friend burn for her sins but Richard was a man of his word. He knew one way or the other justice would soon catch up with her. He knew he would deliver her the news and the watch anytime soon. Three days ago, he had fulfilled his end of the bargain. Now it was up to her to guess the magic words and save her life. Only she could save herself. The confessions were the easy part as predicted by detective Jesse. Third day now the first magic word was the talk of the day geographical location.

The detective felt like crying as the doctor struggled to put the pieces together. It was not just a matter of saying the magic word. A link; the place or coordinates were needed to unlock the system somehow.

"Think doctor let's look at this from a different angle. What do you have in common with this killer?"

"I don't know. We met because of his son."

"Let's see, son, death, life, pain, sorrow, apology,"

"Sorry could be the first magic word. He shot me already what will he gain if I die? What can make him change his mind?"

"Forgiveness."

"Where is the watch? Turn it on. Let's see if this works."

Minutes passed by before they tried the first magic word.

"Sorry", shouted the doctor.

"Correct magic word but wrong geographical position. Please enter the correct coordinates."

"Where did you first meet? For the very first time."

"In my office at the hospital."

"Jump in the car lets go."

The two jumped in the car as fast as they can. People looked in shock until the detective switched on the blue emergency lights in front of his car. Other cars gave way as the car headed to the hospital. They arrived and parked just next to the entrance door away from the car park. They left the car doors opened and entered inside straight into the lift and to the level above. Frantically the doctor searched for the keys and then struggled to insert the correct key despite having done that for years. The door opened, and they both looked at the watch breathing heavily. A message soon was displayed on the screen. A circle appeared on the watch for seconds.

"Correct magic word and correct geolocation. Please wait system reverting to previous settings."

After a while there was a beeping sound from the watch. The system was reset. The doctor hugged the detective and cried like a baby. Minutes later a constant beeping sound caught their attention. They shot each other a quick glance.

"What is it now? We still have three more days to find the remaining magic words."

A message was displayed on the screen.

"Count down initiated you have twelve hours to enter the magic words and reset the system before shutdown."

The doctor looked as if she had seen a ghost and stubbed the detective with her eyes.

"Damn! Son of a beast! He should have just killed me in cold blood. Why he said seven days when it's just bloody twelve hours."

The doctor sat down and cried.

"I think once you entered the first magic word you will have twelve hours to complete the rest."

"Don't be a smart ass. You are enjoying every minute seeing me suffer?"

"Hey, don't blame me what did I do? I was not there when you were butchering his son."

"Correct magic word; butchering. Now link this magic word to correct geolocation. You have thirty minutes for this task."

"Where is this location?"

Questioned the detective.

The doctor looked at the detective and suddenly got up and the two ran out of the office toward the operating rooms pushing people out of the way.

"Excuse us! Excuse us!"

The two ran in the corridors and stairs until they have reached the operating rooms.

"Is this the room?"

"I don't know?"

"What do you mean you don't know? Did you not operate on his son?"

"It wasn't me. I hired a consulted who is now dead."

"I don't understand. So, what does he what from you? What did you do wrong?"

"I delegated the task therefore accountable according to him. He said that Juniors reflect the image of the senior. The senior was aware of all the wrong doing yet he went on to allow it to happen."

"Damn he is crazier than I thought."

After a while they entered another operating room.

"It must have been this one. Repeat the magic word again."

"Butchering." Shouted the detective.

They both looked at the watch and waited for the OK confirmation.

A beeping sound was let off. They were both holding the watch together with their heads joined together looking at the watch.

"Correct magic word and geolocation but wrong voice synthesis patterns."

"Son of a beast! What does that mean?"

Shouted the doctor.

"Wait, a minute. You said the first magic word. I said the second magic word and now I said the third magic word. OK I think it's now your turn?"

"My turn? Are you saying if I was on my own I could have not reached this far?"

"One way to find out. Go on let's see."

The doctor hesitated but later gathered her courage.

"Butchering."

A beeping sound set all on alert.

A system resetting in progress message is displayed on the screen. They looked at each other while both holding the watch together. This time the watch started flashing just after resetting it. The automatically requesting the last magic word to set everything to normal. The countdown began shortly after another thirty minutes. Time was running out. It was not even the initial twelve hours proposed but a mere thirty minutes was all they had. They looked at each other. The doctor looked exhausted and pale. This time there was no time to relax. This was more frightening. This could be the end of her. Fail the magic word failing to find the correct location then the game is over.

"We have come this far don't give up now. Get up! Let's go!"

"We need the magic word first. We can't just go maybe it's here too."

"OK let's try again. Brain storm anything that comes to your mind first."

"Money, operation, family, anger, remorseful, mistake, hospital, insurance, accountability, eh?"

She didn't finish the sentence as a beeping sound went off. They looked puzzled and joyful. It didn't seem to be very complicated. All three magic words with time to spare. The big question was where being this geolocation.

"Yes! But where? Think. What does he want? Accountable for what?"

"I don't know. Accountable for my actions. Eh let's see. I think I know. We need to go to the court. I was not in the court."

They both looked at each other with sadness.

"Double jeopardy. He shot you once he can't shoot you twice."

The doctor stopped and looked at the detective.

"In fact, he shot me twice. First in the court and secondly in the car park."

"No wait a minute. He shot eh, Dr. Maurice."

"No, he shot me as Dr. Maurice and shot me again in the car park. Ah no! I am going to die. He is replaying his first plan the one I out-smarted I think now he is correcting what should have been. Son of a beast. I told them that this bastard is way ahead of me. Take him down but they played down my fears. I am a respectable doctor. I don't deserve this. We can't stop research just because someone's son died. We sacrifice one to save hundreds that's life. I have history to support me. The bastard is just going to finish his plan and correct his first mistake. I am going to die in court. All this, is a booby trap a means to his plan. Damn! I feel like I am a fool."

"Get up Doctor. We are running of time. Better to die in court defending what you believe in than to day here. Let's go."

The two ran downstairs and out of the hospital and straight into the car left outside near the entrance. There was silence as the car headed to the court in the city with twenty-five minutes left. The detective held the doctor's hand briefly trying to comfort her. Surely if it was any other day, the doctor would be screaming and shouting for the detective to reduce the speed and drive normally but there was a lot at stake. In fact, she wished that she would die in a car accident than face what the killer had in store for her. She recalled the day he shot her in the car park. Surely, she felt the pain and up to now she has flashbacks of that day. Fear was more terrifying than death itself she reckoned. The detective did what he does best. All those extending defensive driving course lessons were paying off. If he was not a policeman, he could have collided with another car by now but he was still cruising over 100km/h. The car was shaking and vibrating as he headed to the other side of the city. Beating traffic lights and sometimes passing through red lights the detective made it to court with seventeen minutes to spare. They both jumped off, but the doctor was reluctant. She wiped tears running down her cheeks. The detective waited for her for a while.

"We are running out of time. Hurry up,"

"I am dying anywhere. What's the hurry?"

The detective tried to open the court door, but the door was locked he quickly pushed slightly the doctor to the side.

"Stand back."

He jumped into the car and knocked the door down. Quickly the two were inside the court. They took out the watch, and they both said the magic word.

"Accountability!"

They shouted.

They waited for the response. They hugged each other waiting.

"Correct magic word but incorrect geo-locational place."

The doctor screamed and cursed clenching her fist.

"Bastard! I knew it. He cheated me. He brought me here so I die here. I out smarted you once! You coward! You spineless son of a beast! Who is the murderer now?"

The detective paced up and down pushing his hair backward.

"Accountability, and it's not in the court so where would this be? Unless."

"Unless what detective?"

"Unless it's accountability for his son? Quickly jump in the car lets go?"

"Where are we going?"

"Just jump in the car we have less than twelve minutes left."

This was a do or die situation for the doctor. The detective knew that the life of the doctor was now in his hands. If all this was for real, this was the last chance she had. He had a gut feeling that this was the only place that made sense. Another defensive driving challenge a twenty-minute journey in ten minutes. It was now getting dark, and the roads were getting busier. The only way was to take short cuts through roads with less traffic. Luckily there was a shortcut. The doctor looked scared. Probably last ten minutes of her life. Five minutes into the journey the doctor started asking questions.

"It seems we are just driving where exactly are we going?"

"Just wait and see. I am praying to God that this is the correct place otherwise I don't know how I will forgive myself."

Overtaking other cars and nearly colliding with oncoming traffic had become a routine even though the journey was less than ten minutes. The car crashed the wooden gate to the cemetery, and the detective turned the steering wheel sending a cloud of dust into the air. The car continued hitting crosses on top of the grave and throwing the doctor and the detective from side to side and up and down as it moved over some graves especially the ones on the edges and corners near the duct road.

"I don't know where his son is buried?"

The detective looked at the doctor and smiled.

"I know where both are buried. I mean where his son is buried and where his fake grave is."

Minutes later they arrived. They jumped out of the car and stood next to the grave and scrolled down the watch and entered the magic word. A message instantly appeared that she was not in the exact location although she was in the vicinity. They both looked at each other. The detective hold the doctors hand and directed her on top of the grave and soon an acknowledging message appeared on the screen. This was the correct position. After a few seconds the system started setting itself up. They both looked at each other and smiled. Soon after there was a beeping sound and a congratulation message appeared on the screen. "

"To finalize this reset please accept the incoming call."

The synchronization message appeared on the screen after the blue-tooth had been automatically activated.

The doctor's phone started ringing. She quickly took her phone out and answered the call. She put the phone to her ear.

"Doctor. Hello. I never thought you will be so determined to find where my son is. Sometimes you just surprise me. I swear I thought you would prefer to die in court fighting for what you believe in. No one has ever done this. Wait, a minute. I set two vocal syntheses access codes. Who was helping you? You are the first. If you are this smart why butcher my son. That was the most stupid thing any person could do."

"So, I can go now?"

"Give me the phone let me talk to him."

Requested the detective whispering.
"Who else is with you?"
"Can I go now?"
"I said who is with you. Who is helping you?"
"You bastard you are just playing games with me. I did not kill your son. I am tired of your stupid games. I am going."
"Oh, wait a minute."
"What?"
"Say hi to my son for me."

CHAPTER THIRTEEN

A loud sound rocketed throughout the graveyard. It happened like in slow motion. The detective was busy think about their journey back home how he saved the doctor from this killer. Suddenly the watch flew up in the sky before being beaten by gravity and falling next to his feet. The doctor still had the phone in her hands which the detective took shortly after instantly holding her as she falls. The sound of a gunshot at close range nearly deafened his ears. Blood spurted out onto his face covering him all over. Instincts kicked in and he fell on his knees with the doctor in his hands onto the top of the killer's son's grave. She just looked at him and all her breath instantaneously disappeared. The detective tried to cover the bullet hole next to her chest. Blood was gushing out and in a few seconds, it seemed all blood had been drained out into the killer's son's grave. The detective drenched in blood cried profusely before reaching for the phone.

"I am going to kill you. I have seen your face a thousand times. Every time I blink I see you. I remembered you. You stole my evidence, a bullet casing at the conference room building. That belonged to me. You will pay for all the people you have killed. No one is above the law."

"You motherfucker do you know who you are talking to? I spared your life just because my son wanted to be a detective. You are threatening me maybe I send you to my son now. I have the coordinates right here."

The detective ducked and remained quiet for a while looking around.

"Too much blood on your hands."

"Wait until you have seen what I did to the Vice President?"

"What have you done? If you touch her, I will kill you myself. She is a good person. You kill her and you are dead meat."

"Look behind you." Said Richard laughing uncontrollably.

The detective instantly looked backwards and saw an SUV parked in the woods off the cemetery.

"Sharp shooter I never miss. Instant death or you want to save another life. Hm you make me laugh. You think you know what is going on? They are all corrupt. I will purge all and bring new blood. I was hoping that maybe I spare you but that woman has corrupted you. You threaten me you, Douchebag standing on top of my son's grave. I swear I will murder you right now in cold blood. Don't push me. I could have smoked you a long time ago. You were not in the operating room. You don't know what happened there. I was there. Look beneath you.

That's my boy there. My own flesh and blood. They butchered him like he was a dog. You heard the doctor boosting about sacrificing one to save a hundred. That's my son you are talking about. My boy. Like the doctor, I will sacrifice hundred to save one. They can't do that to my boy. What more proof you need? Look underneath your feet?"

"Even if they killed your son, you can't take the law into your own hands."

The detective heard Richard cursing continuously. Silence broke out.

"When are you going to put her down, she is gone? OK you want to play. What is the magic word? You have seven days. Keep her watch and keep her phone too."

The line went dead after that and the SUV reversed and headed toward the main road away from the cemetery. The detective covered in blood looked at the doctor for a while and when he was about to get up a bullet casing fell from the sky. He picked it up before throwing it back to the ground and licking his fingers.

"Very sorry. I should have left you at the court. Very sorry. You should have died at the court at least defending what you believe in."

He placed her down on top of the killer's son's grave. He picked up the watch and ran to his car. He jumped in and chased after the killer. A huge cloud of dust rose into the sky. Even though it was getting dark dust clouds rose in the skies as the detective chased the black SUV. The detective's car joined the road from the dusty cemetery road. He knew the killer was never to let him go once he had marked him. His aim now was to kill him too. All his efforts were to no avail the doctor died anywhere. He stepped on the gas pedal and drove like a rally driver overtaking and sometimes driving on the hard shoulder. The drivers of the cars sounded their horns after he had swiftly passed them. Richard expected the detective to start worrying about his own life but when he looked into the rear-view mirror, he knew he had company. After the chase a sudden bang to the back of the SUV sends the black SUV jerking and causing Richard to lose control of the car. The sound of the horn of the oncoming car caused Richard to adjust and quickly swerve back into his correct lane. The very time the detective's car smashed on the back of the SUV Richard's watch beeped but he had no time to look at it until he felt warm blood on his side stomach. He knew he was in a different geo-locational space-time continuum. He had gone back to the time he was shot dead. He quickly scrolled down his watch and entered new coordinates. The time he raised his head he had moved to the other lane in front of oncoming traffic. A huge lorry sounded the hoarse trumpet scaring Richard for a while. He drove even further to the other side of the road after having his SUV scratched on the side by the lorry. Quickly he moved back to his position. He touched his side stomach and noticed that he was now badly bleeding. He looked at the watch and saw a message that read;

"Movement in space and time continuum is nearly complete new coordinates entered accepted. Few seconds left please wait."

Another crash from the back and a gunshot sends Richard ducking and swerving in front of oncoming traffic.

After a while a beep sound and a message on the watch confirmed that movement in space-time continuum was completed. The bleeding stopped. Richard touched his stomach and smiled. He picked up the phone.

"The Vice President needs you, Hero. Don't waste time. Bye."

The SUV suddenly started firing on all cylinders and soon started opening the gap. Slowly and slowly the detective started realizing that this day was not his. He understood that he had more issues at hand than the killer. He conceded that the killer at least today he had spared his life. He now had more issue at hand.

Richard arrived at his in-laws and parked the car in the garage and through the garage door entered the house straight to the guest house area. He knocked at the door and instantly his wife opened the door. They hugged and kissed. She was very happy to see him.

"I am very glad you came back. I was scared that I will never see you again."

"I am happy to see you too."

The couple talked about a lot of stuff. Richard talked about his adventure as well but kept getting stuck here and there.

"You don't seem yourself what is wrong did something bad happen to you? You seem okay to me apart from this distraction."

"I am okay. Just not sure about something."

"You can tell me you know."

"I know but I am not sure if that correct or not see how I sleep tonight."

Later that night Richard entered coordinates into his watch and synchronized with his gadget. When his wife had fallen asleep, he opened his old bag and took out precision knives, disinfectants and some cotton swabs and cotton wool. He placed all this on the table and some rubber gloves. He looked at his watch and slept. Katherine had a dream. They were out doors and they were swimming with Richard and her parents were in a distance having a picnic. They swarm for some time before Richard got out of the swimming pool leaving her in the pool. She placed her arm in the water and felt the warm water. She can't tell how long she was in the pool alone. The time she looked up Richard and her parents had gone. She panicked and got out of the water. She looked around and shouted for Richard.

"Darling, where are you?"

She shouted. She looked around and found out that she was naked. Her clothes were gone. She looked around. When she heard voices, she ducked in the water. She looked to see who it was only to find out that it was Richard and her dad.

"Katherine! Katherine! Where are you? Katherine! Let's go back home. Katherine!"

As she was about to answer she woke up and switched the side headboard light.

"Oh, my God. What happened? Darling wake up."

Richard was bleeding on his side and moving his head in his sleep. He was asleep but underneath his eyelids his eyes were moving.

"Richard! Richard! Wake up."

She tried waking him up, but he was in a deep sleep. She looked on the side table and saw the medical instruments. She touched the side that was bleeding searching for the wound. It seemed her thumb finger pressed on the bullet wound. He squinted with pain but did not wake up. He was losing blood fast. She had to act immediately. She got up and went to her parent's bedroom. She woke them up and brought them to the guest room bedroom.

Richard woke up screaming in pain.

"Hold him down!"

Shouted Richard's mother-in-law.

Katherine and her father held Richard's arms and legs pinning him down while she removed the bullet. Richard fell asleep after. After a while Richard woke up to find her mother-in-law sitting next to him and his wife and his dad holding his legs and hands.

"It's alright. It's going to be okay."

Said mother-in-law.

"You will be okay, Darling. Mother removed the bullet."

At first Richard looked lost and as it sunk in he looked around.

"Where is my watch and my gadget?"

Katherine pointed at the table and Richard tried to get up and take the watch but screamed in pain touching the side stomach that had now been bandaged.

"I will get that for you Darling."

Katherine's parents disappeared before he thanked them. Quickly he scrolled on the watch and entered some coordinates soon afterward he fell asleep. Katherine didn't notice. Richard never slept early. Katherine on most cases would fall asleep first. She sat next to him and kept talking until she fell asleep as well. In the city, it's business as usual. The Vice President's limo parked outside her office building and the bodyguards got out first and looked around before the Vice President got out and entered the building. This was not like her. Over the years, she had loved the limelight spending more time with the reporters and photographers outside. Something big had happened to her and it seemed to have shattered her confidence. Or it was just a matter of a lot of pressing issues on the agenda. The country had lost confidence in the leadership. No one really knew who was behind the deaths of so many government officials. There was a killer lurking around. Everywhere there was extra security. Gone were the days where government officials paraded themselves in public. The magic word killer was running rampant terrorizing the American way of life. Rumors had it that the Magic-word killer had a very long to-do-list and somehow that list included most government ministers, law makers, doctors and even the President, but no one knew for sure. Only one person knew exactly who was on the list and this person was the killer himself. No one knew if this was a hoax or not but one thing was for sure. The people were really dying. Most believed that an underground movement had established itself killing officials in the name of the deceased campaigner murdered in court months back. Whoever was behind this was more dangerous than they thought. Some called him the delayed-time killer. He would shoot someone and tell them that they will die in seven days and all died in that time. The Vice President entered her office and looked around. She walked next to the windows and opened the curtain. She removed her jacket and dialed a number. She paced left and right in her office.

"Come on pick up the phone."

She shouted to herself. The phone ran for some time before the Professor answered.

"Yes Mrs. Vice President."

"Professor what's your final stance regarding the incident."

There was silence for a while. The Professor breathed heavily before he answered.

"My personal view would be that he was bluffing. I checked his body functions at the time and to me this being just my own personal view he was more scared of you but respectful in some way. Harming you I think is out of the question. He was not upset in any way for the few minutes that you had. So, to answer your question I think he didn't shoot you."

"Why would he ask about the magic-word from me? Why would he give me this watch? All the people he had given this watch to are all dead?"

"He wants something from you or he thinks he might need a favor from you in the future."

"A favor from me? Since when did I dine with killers and murderers?"

"Let me look at his file that might shade more light."

There was a moment of silence.

"If he had shot you Mrs. Vice President what would you do? If there was that option that he can reverse this what would you do?"

"I like the way you are putting this through. You are sure he did not shoot me? I am dead worried thinking that the killer smoked me. I think there is one way to find out. OK thank you Professor."

Miles away in the city park just after the big shopping center. A car arrived and parked nearby. A young lady got out and opened the back-seat door. A young boy probably five or six years old jumped out of the car. The woman reached for a bag on the seat and closed the car doors. She alarmed the car, and the two walked toward the park. They arrived on one of the park benches and sat down. After having something to eat the woman took out a remote-controlled toy car and handed the remote to her son who welcomed it with much delight. The women took ear phones and started listening to the music while watching her son play. That went on for some time until the music stopped and an incoming call message was displayed on the handset.

"Hello. Subject on its way get into position."

The lady stood up and looked around before going to her son. She took the remote control from her son and sent the car toward a woman who was approaching from the road leading to the car park. The woman from the city mall car park was Katherine. She looked worried as she walked toward the woman with her son. As she closed in a toy car crossed her path. She looked at it and then at the women and her son. She stopped and looked at the boy. He looked like her son. The boy suddenly ran toward her. For a moment she got confused, she had a flashback of the time her own son reacted the same way on seeing her. A van suddenly appeared from the corner heading toward them. The toy car jumped onto the main road and crossed part of the road. Katherine looked at the van heading toward them, she looked at the toy car that was already in the road in the path of the van. She looked at the boy as he crossed in front of her. Motherly instincts kicked in and she screamed and shouted for the boy to stop but the boy continued and she had to act. She ran toward the boy. The boy knelt in the road to pick up the toy car that had stopped in the middle of the road. The van screeched its tires as it tried to stop and Katherine stepped on the road. The van halted just a few feet away from the boy who stood up and looked at the van that nearly hit him. Instantly the boy looked shocked with his eyes wide open. He dropped the toy car and cried as the van stopped just in front of him. He ran toward his mother leaving the car in the road. The van's side door opened. Katherine picked up the car and looked at the boy instantly two men got out of the van and carried her inside as she wriggled her legs.

"Put me down. What do you think you are doing? Help!"

She fought the men, but they over powered her. The van's door closed and the screeching of tire sound made the boy cry even more. As the van disappeared around the next corner. The toy car was left in the middle of the road. The lady and her son got up and walked toward the road just before a car came from the corner and left the toy car squashed to the road surface. The boy after seeing this cried even louder. The lady carried her son in her arms and looked in the direction the van had gone. Katherine after being blindfolded was dragged into this building. It smelled like a factory but she could hear a generator making noise from a distance she was untied and as soon as her tied hands were freed she removed the cloth covering her eyes. She looked around. There were boxes around and the room had no windows but a small air vent on top. She started hitting the door pulling the handle, but the door was locked. Later in the evening the Vice President was still in her office. She sat down and switched the flat screen on the wall on. She switched to the channel news. There was a reporter reading the news.

"This just in. Two government officials have reported coming face to face with the Magic-word killer they both claimed to have been given a watch after being shot. This increased the number of the victims to over a hundred in less than two months. Right now, they are frantically asking anyone for help with the magic-words. When put in such a position it seems it is more traumatizing than what these people are depicting. The killer or killers are still on the run. Unidentified sources close to the government insisted that the killer was dead. One of the copycat killers was shot after killing one of the special unit officer. The President just yesterday announced a huge reward for the capture of this killer. Rachel reporting for Touchladybird lucky news."

The ringing sound of her phone alarmed her. She looked at the incoming number and answered quickly. The person on the other hand only spoke one or two words before the line went dead. The Vice President forced a smile for a while. She seemed worried still. This was not her. Ever since meeting the killer she had preferred not to talk too much with people, she otherwise would communicate with. This phone call at least brought some sense of relief to her. Surely, she had some unfinished business and time was running out for her, or was it? Forty minutes passed, and she was still in her office watching the news. There was a knock on the door before she replied one of her bodyguard opened the door and peeped inside.

"It's time let's go."

The Vice President looked at him and smiled.

"Not yet."

She replied looking at her watch.

Another half an hour went by without anything special just news of the killers havoc he was causing. She looked at her watch and switched off the flat screen. A beeping sound sends her panicking and looking around. She opened her hand bag and saw the watch given to her by the killer flashing. She looked at it for a while her heart beating very fast. She picked up the watch and read the flashing message.

"I should have killed you. First my son now my wife. You will regret this."

She scrolled down the phone and another beep sound went off. There was another message this time a system message.

"Synchronizing in progress please wait."

After a while her phone started ringing. A bit shocked and surprised she picked up the phone and looked at the caller. The caller was using an unknown caller identification. Hesitantly she replied.

"Hello."

"Bring back my wife or you are dead meat."

The man sounded really upset she could hear the animal rage in his hoarse voice.

The Vice President laughed for a while softly.

"You think this is funny?"

"Do you want to play? What is the magic-word?"

"What?"

Asked the man surprised and confused.

"Only me can be the master of that game you have no idea. No idea at all."

"How does that feel you think you are smart, hey? I will take your wife with me?"

There was a moment of silence and the man cursed in the background.

"I should have killed you. Maybe I was wrong about you after all?"

"What?"

Shouted the Vice President surprised. She paused for a while.

"I thought you killed me already?"

"I was bluffing."

There was a moment of silence too. The Vice President stood up and walked to the window she smiled. She felt like she has been given a second chance.

"Listen. I am the Vice President we met weeks ago. Are you sure about this?"

"Why would I lie to you?"

"You lied in the first place."

"Self-defense. Would you have let me go?"

The Vice President took time to reply.

"I guess you are right. I thought you killed me. Okay, I believe you I will let her go straight away. I thought you killed me."

There was silence.

"Keep your word let her go home we suffered enough already. Bye."

"I will."

The Vice President phoned the Professor straight away. In the lab, the Professor was sat on his chair. He had a glass of red wine in his hand. He was watching the news. Although he was sure the killer might not have killed the Vice President, there was another nagging feeling that what if he did? That meant that all his dreams and efforts would be to waste. No one had the guts and determination to take on a project like this. Even the President had distanced himself from such a huge task. The phone rung and quickly he picked up the phone and answered it fearing for the worst.

"Professor you were right after all. He confessed he was bluffing."

Without saying anything the Professor shouted rejoicing and celebrating.

"I was distraught all day, where are you? Are you at your office I will come and see you?"

"There is something else I have to do first. Meet after when I get back okay."

Soon after the line went dead.

A van and three dark SUVs were parked outside a huge building. Inside were the special unit personnel. There was Viktor, Nikolai, Brenton, Claudio, Dwain and Elvis. While they were talking Dwain's cell phone rang.

"OK,".

Dwain replied and ended the call.

"Who was it?"

Asked Brenton.

"Vice President. Let her go."

"Are you sure about this? This woman has seen our faces?"

"That's what she said."

"Do what the Vice President asked you to do that was an order."

The door of one of the SUVs was opened and Claudio walked to the van and opened the door. He entered inside with the rest except for Viktor. After a while Viktor left the SUV and entered the van. Now all the men in one place, they started talking.

"Rumors has it that the Vice President has meetings with the killer."

"Who told you that?"

"Just know I have very reliable sources who can confirm this. The word on the street is that the killer shot her and now she is trying to use the killer's wife as a bargaining tool."

"What are you saying?"

"I think to release this woman would put us at greater risk. She is compromised now. How can we trust her, she had a meeting with the killer the same day Sydney was shot dead by the killer? I say we hold on to this woman until we are through with him. For Sydney."

"I don't think it's a clever idea. We disobey the order and we are all finished."

"What if the killer really shot her? He might come after us after she has died."

Suggested Elvis.

"I say we just tell her that we let her go but leave her for a week and find out what will happen."

 One sunny day a limousine cruised toward the city center. It was another beautiful day and people were going their way as it was business as usual for most. The Vice President was in the limousine nearly two weeks after the first encounter with the killer. Everything turned out to be okay after all. She knew it was like a second chance in life. She quickly got out of the limo and posed for the reporters and photographers. Reporters ran to her.

"Mrs. Vice President we believe the killer at one point shot you and it's more than seven days how did you manage that?"

The Vice President looked everywhere and posed for the photographers.

"I established a research lab and poured in a lot of money most of which was my personnel money. Today I can proudly say that we have achieve a milestone. We have managed to give each one of you a serial number that is uniquely linked to your DNA. This has enabled us to achieve a lot and improve security. The day I had an encounter with the killer we managed to delay time and change geolocation into another time-space vacuum. In other words, I was with him but at the time he shot me I had been given a new geographical location. When he shot me I was not there? I was somewhere in time and space. That can only be achieved through assigning serial numbers and linking this to individual DNA. Now you will see why I was saying that it is compulsory for everyone to have a serial number and have their DNA taken."

The Vice President felt a billion dollars. Another report asked her a question. That very instance the Vice President thought that she saw someone within the crowd who scared her that she hid behind her bodyguard. Everyone looked where she was looking. She looked scared and frightened.

"What is it?"

Asked the bodyguard.

The Vice President looked as if she had seen a ghost.

"Nothing."

She replied.

"OK thank you for your time."

She left the gathering and entered the office building. For the first time, she insisted the bodyguard stayed with her. She sat in her chair and soon afterward stood up and walked toward the window. The upper window was open. She looked among the crowds for some time searching but she could not find anyone. At last she convinced herself that she might be seeing things but still insisted that the bodyguard stayed.

Minutes later a man stood at the window on the balcony. The Vice President's initial reaction was to scream and the bodyguard instantly stood in front of her looking at the man at the window. A red light reflected inside and aimed on the chest of the bodyguard. In what appeared to be in slow motion the bodyguard traced the red light from the window to his chest. Instantly the noise of the breaking glass made him panic. He looked at his chest but he was okay. His hand pushed the Vice President to the ground. He looked at the man as the man disappeared from the balcony. The Vice President got up and looked at the bodyguard. He was okay there was no blood or any wound but for some time he looked lost and disoriented.

"Are you okay? Are you shot?"

"I can't tell I don't know what happened. He fired a shot. The window was smashed to pieces."

Just before he finished talking a bullet casing dropped from nowhere onto the middle of his legs. He slowly knelt and picked up the bullet casing. The Vice President looked on, her heart beating very fast. This was déjà vu. She knew the feeling and confusion. The bodyguard lifted the hot bullet casing with much easy. He did not react to the temperature of the casing but the bullet left marks on his hands. He looked at the casing and looked at the Vice President with a face that seemed to ask her what on earth had just happened? The Vice President walked slowly toward the window. She pushed the curtain to one side and looked for the killer first before leaning against the window. She looked everywhere, but the killer was gone. She looked in the gardens outside for any shadows before walking back to the table. She switched on the flat television and watched the news. "This just in a woman has been found dead today dumped in the street with a bullet hole in her head. It is believed that it was the widow of the presumed Magic-word killer. Police are treating her death as suspicious."

CHAPTER FOURTEEN

The voice screams were heard coming from the Vice President's office. The Vice President felt her stomach moving and felt all her energies drained. At first, she did not look at her bodyguard after he screamed too. She assumed it was because of the shock on hearing the death of the killer's wife. It was seconds later that she had a huge thump noise. She looked behind her only to find the bodyguard breathing his last breath covered in blood with blood popping out his chest. She cursed and cried trying very hard to stop the bleeding. The bodyguard looked at her and smiled before dying. The Vice President still kneeling looked at the bodyguard and then at her hands which were covered in blood. She got up and walked to her office cabinet. She opened the cabinet and took keys to her drawer. She opened the drawer and took out a small box. Inside was a gun and a bullet magazine. She loaded the gun and removed the safety pin. She walked toward the window and looked outside. Richard looked at his watch and scrolled down he took out a gadget from his pocket and programmed it to search for numbers in the vicinity. The gadget picked up about five cell phone numbers. He phoned one of the phones.

"Hello."

"Who killed my wife?"

"Who is this? How did you get my number?"

"Your worst enemy."

The man placed the phone down and ducked.

"We have company the killer is nearby I guess!"

He shouted. The men went outside with guns and scanned the area. They looked far down the road and saw an SUV parked down the road with its engine running. Instantly a man got out of the car wearing a baseball cap and some dark clothes. He started walking toward the building. A beeping sound went off causing him to stand for a while in one place. The other man took cover. He started walking approaching the men and started shooting as he approached. A bullet nearly caught him and he stopped and keyed in some coordinates before a message was displayed.

"Please wait movement in space-time continuum in progress."

The man looked at his watch and looked ahead before aiming a shot at the man approaching. He did not shoot but waited for the man to appear. The man did not show any fear. He came forward holding a gun and aiming this at the killer.

The men were near of each other when a beep sound made the killer to lose focus only to be shot on the shoulder. The other man was Brenton. A member of the special unit squad and best friend of the murdered special unit squad member Sydney.

"You took my friend I took your wife we are even." Shouted Brenton.

Richard felt a tear running down his left cheek. Instantly as soon as there was confirmation that the movement in space-time continuum was complete. Richard aimed his gun at Brenton and fired continuous shots sending Brenton ducking. To Brenton's surprise the man kept coming in the open without fear. He had never seen anyone like him. He advanced like an angry lion without fear and with courage. Brenton for a while felt a cold shiver of fear running down his spine. He understood why this man had terrorized the whole country. He was determined to send the whole government to the grave. He had never met someone with such determination. He was an animal. Humans tend to possess fear as well, but this man was more than a vicious beast. Brenton got up and fired a shot. The only thing Richard did was to look at his watch. A bullet, it seemed lodged into Richard's shoulder. A loud scream sent Brenton ducking. The scream was made by someone in his group, precisely by Viktor. He looked backward and was frightened by the voice of Elvis on the radio.

"Man down. I repeat."

Brenton looked at Richard who kept coming and talked to Elvis.

"What happened mate?"

"Dwain is down. Shot on the shoulder,"

"What? Who shoot him? Is someone else there?"

"I don't know what happened."

Brenton crawled back to his friends. On arrival, he found his friend holding his shoulder bleeding badly. He looked further down and saw Richard coming fearless and determined to eliminate all. Now, he knew what was happening. The others took cover and aimed at Richard. They fired bullets at Richard and behind them Viktor groaned in pain and died. They all looked at each other and retreated. They surrounded Viktor who was already dead his body riddled with bullet holes. Richard stopped after a message was displayed on his watch. He entered different coordinates and waited. After the coordinates were successfully confirmed Nikolai rose and tried to run. Richard stopped and aimed before firing two consecutive shots. Nikolai staggered forward before falling to the ground. Brenton the strongest of the group stood up and fired a shot at Richard and the next thing he knew Elvis was on the floor clutching his neck.

"Please don't shoot him I took the bullet for him." Explained Elvis.

Brenton looked confused and aimed at Richard as he approached. He fired a shot and blood spurts out covering Claudio's face. Elvis breathed his last breath. This time it was a do or die situation. Brenton looked at the coming Richard and looked at all the man who were dead. It was just him and Claudio left. Richard was too close for comfort. Brenton looked around and aimed the gun at Richard but instantly Claudio screamed shouting at Brenton to stop.

"Don't shoot him otherwise I am the one who will be shot."

Brenton paused for a while thinking how to handle this situation. Instantly he pointed the gun at Claudio and looked at Richard's reaction. Richard playing mind games stopped. Brenton smiled and looked first at Richard and then at Claudio. A bullet pierced through the head of Claudio. In slow motion Claudio fell to the ground. Brenton quickly looked at Richard who remained standing. Shocked and saddened that the killer was still standing and breathing when he had expected him to die. Richard smiled and kept moving forward aiming the gun at Brenton. Confused, now he didn't know how to react. Richard smiled as he approached with a gun raised and aimed at Brenton. Brenton looked at all his dead friends he realized that to shoot Richard would mean his death. Brenton was much stronger than Richard. Brenton thought that Richard will deliberately let him shoot him but instead commit suicide. So, Brenton thought fast and thinking that he was the genius one pulled the gun and aimed at Richard as he approached. But as he had expected Richard did not react he waited for Brenton's move first. So, Brenton smiled and looked at Richard.

"Your friend was a soldier. He deserved to die but my wife was a civilian you had no right to take her away from me. You die today."

"Wrong you die first."

Brenton pointed a gun at Richard at close range and looked in his eyes. Brenton did not see any reaction from Richard. His eyes were the eyes of the devil. They were red and unblinking. Brenton when he looked at Richard's face he couldn't tell whether this man was afraid to die or not. Maybe anger disguised his reactions. The two men were locked in the same position and stance both aiming guns at each other. They walked clockwise looking into each other's eyes. A beeping sound from Richard's watch went off and Richard lowered his gun. Instantly Brenton aimed the gun at himself and pulled the trigger shooting himself.

He took a quick breath and looked shocked as if he had expected Richard to fall to the ground.

"No."

Shouted Brenton touching his chest and falling to the ground.

Richard walked to where he laid on the ground and raised his gun.

"You are a tricking bastard you tricked me. You bloody coward."

"Say hi to my wife."

A bullet shattered Brenton's brains scattering them onto the ground.

 The Vice President walked out of the bathroom in her office and straight into her limousine and the limo drove off. The President after hearing the news of the death of the killer's widow visited the Vice President's office looking for her. The door was not locked. He entered inside as he heard the noise made by the television as the news channel was on. He noticed that a bodyguard was lying on the floor. He waked toward him and knelt. He touched his body checking if he was still breathing. The office door opened while he was still kneeling and thinking that it was the Vice President spoke first without looking at the person who had just entered the office.

"What is going on around here?"

Said the President turning to face the person who had just entered the office. The man who had just entered was Richard who had a gun in his hand.

"Who are you? What do you want?"

"The Magic-word killer."

"Really, I thought he was dead."

"Why did you kill my wife?"

"I had no clue. Nothing to do with your wife."

Richard looked at the face of the President and saw that he was telling the truth. The President instantly withdrew his gun and pointed at Richard.

"Son you kill my bodyguard you die too."

He instantly pulled the trigger shooting Richard who just looked on and touched his chest. Instantly a beeping sound went off from his watch. The Vice President was in the limousine when a beeping sound went off she looked at the watch. There was a message.

"Movement in space-time continuum back to office coordinates,"

The President instantly touched his chest and fell on his knees. He looked at Richard who was down. The gun from his hand fell to the ground. Richard raised his head.

"Who shoot you?"

Richard asked the President.

The President did not say anything he looked behind him to see who had shot him but there was no one. A body guard came in running after hearing the gunshot and aimed a gun at Richard while attending to the President.

"You shot the President. Why?"

"I didn't."

"Yes, you did."

"Ask him he is the one who shot me."

He checked his pulse.

"He is dead."

Shouted the bodyguard. Richard cursed and lifted the gun but without the intention to shot the bodyguard. The bodyguard fired two consecutive shots one in the chest and the other in the head and the gun that was in Richard's hand fell onto the floor. While the guard

was still attending to the President, a bullet casing fell on his head. He looked into the air and on the ceiling and picked up the bullet casing. He cursed and dropped the casing down before taking out a handkerchief and picking up the bullet casing.
"Where did this come from?"
He looked around in astonishment. A lady was swimming on the beach enjoying the sun and the warm temperature waters. She swam underneath the water and then resurfaced. She looked around and at the beach as a friend of hers was sat there looking at her. The woman in the water signaled to her friend on the beach to come to her. After a while the other lady was still in the water. The sound of the phone ringing alerted the woman on the beach. At first, she ignored the phone, but the phone kept ringing. She stood up wearing a light blue bikini with a well-toned body. She wriggled her perfect body as she walked to her friend's sunbed. She picked up her hand bag and took out her phone. She looked at the displayed caller identification and looked toward the sea. For a split second, she thought that her friend had disappeared but on second look she saw her friend resurfacing.
"Harper it's for you!"
Shouted Scarlett.
 Harper swum close to her friend.
"I am on vacation no calls remember?"
"Sounds important the person can't stop calling."
"OK. I am coming."
Harper swum to the shoreline. She got up and walked on the beach revealing her gorgeous body wearing a tight bikini. Her back was covered with her wet long blond hair. She arrived on her sunbed and took her long towel and squeezed out the water from her hair.

The phone was still ringing with nearly seven missed calls in the background.

"Harper speaking."

She listened for a while rubbing her hair with one hand looking at her friend and raising her eyebrows.

"Like I said I am on vacation and I can't."

"Its important. Something big has come up cut the short you are urgently required here."

She frowned for a while before putting the phone down.

"I guess the fun is over something big has happened. I guess I have to go."

The two ladies looked at each other speechless.

Harper arrived at a house in one of the suburb. She got off her Land rover Evoque and rung the gate bell.

"Yes. How can we help you?"

"I want to ask a few questions about your daughter Katherine and her husband if you don't mind."

Instantly the gate opened and Harper entered the yard. The house was a big modern family house with another attached guest house at the back. She stopped for a moment and looked at the guest house at the back. Suddenly the front door opened, and a lady stood at the door.

"Come on in."

Harper looked around and walked to a picture on the wall.

"Very beautiful daughter you got there."

Katherine's mum Isabella looked at the picture before looking down. Tears ran down her cheeks.

"It feels like yesterday when she was here. One day she went shopping and never came back. It was so traumatizing that I thought of killing myself too."

There was a moment of silence. Andrew, Katherine's father entered the lounge room and sat next to his wife.

"What do you know about her death? Did she have enemies?"

The couple looked at each other for a while.

"It all started after the death of our grandson."

"I understand your daughter and her husband blamed the doctors for this."

"After the operation, he changed completely. I have never seen anything like it."

"What do you mean?"

"The doctors might have damaged his nerves. It was horrendous to watch. He could vibrate. There are evil people out there if you ask me."

"What about the shootings? Did your daughter or son had anything to do with this?"

"Our Son-in-Law died that day in court as well."

The couple looked at each other.

"So why would people think that he is still alive and killing people?"

"People associate themselves with good things good values and good morals. When someone stands up for something like this a few people want to have that forever. When that hero dies, the feeling remains and his life is celebrated even after his death. People still want to hang on to hope. I guess his fans the copycats carried on with his work."

"I will be greatly thankful if you can let me stay where your daughter was staying for a few days while I am in town."

The couple looked at each other. Harper and Isabella later that evening they were having a cup of tea in the lounge room. After the coffee, Harper carried her luggage and followed Isabella. The two women entered the guest house. This was a very beautifully decorated house with a small lounge and a bedroom on the other side and a bathroom. There was a small studio room in the basement.

"This is my daughter's house feel at home if you need any help give us a buzz."

Exhausted after the long flight Harper wanted to take a long bath before going to bed. She left her bags on the bed and walked around the place searching for any clues. After a while she returned to the bedroom and removed her bags into the wall wardrobe. She sat on the bed and opened the drawers. There was female lingerie inside. She looked around and saw some blood stains on the carpet. Quickly she took her bag and took out a cotton swab and a tube. She took out a small bottle with a liquid solution. She poured a little on the swap and rubbed the swab on the stained carpet. She placed the swab into the tube and looked. After that she knelt and looked everywhere. Under the bed, she saw the Elinadeivid brand male boxer shorts. She reached for them and as she was dragging the boxer shorts behind them was a gadget emitting a flicking blue light. She quickly reached for the gadget. She sat on the bed and looked at the gadget. She flicked on some functions from the gadget but a message was displayed on the screen.

"Link and synchronize with the watch to continue."

"What watch?"

She asked herself looking around. Soon a beep sound went off coming from the drawers. She quickly took out Katherine's underwear looking for the watch. Another beep went off this time she knelt and looked under the drawer and saw the watch.

There was a message on the watch.
"Press enter to start synchronizing."
She quickly pressed the Enter function and a please wait message synchronization in progress was displayed. After a while two beep sounds went off one from the watch and the other from the gadget. Astonished and mesmerized she went through both the gadget and the watch after a while she heard someone singing in the shower room. She stood up and looked around scared and confused. She heard a male voice from the shower room singing Oh ladybird bring me love bring me luck by Elinadeivid.
Oh, ladybird bring me love bring me luck
I touched ladybird, and I got lucky
I have seen your face a thousand times.
I remember you stole my heart
I need you tonight
Bring me love bring luck
For I don't want to hang on to nothing
Harper walked toward the shower room door and slide the door open. She heard the male voice singing and she could hear the water running in the shower room. She entered the bathroom confused it felt like it was happening there and there. As she was about to pass the mirror and the sink basin area, she bumped into something and fell to the ground. Somehow it felt like someone was standing there. An invisible person. Soon as the man kept singing in the shower room taking a shower and as his voice increased to a high pitch Harper heard a female voice sobbing softly and the sobbing sound increased as the male's singing pitch increased. Harper scared and confused still on the ground felt tear droplets falling on her arms. She looked at her hands and saw the droplets there.

Suddenly a make-up kit hit the shower floor. She looked around as soon as she had heard the sound. She heard the woman sobbing and walking toward the shower cubicle. The man's voice was at its highest pitch when suddenly the door of the shower cubicle opened. The singing stopped, and the door closed. Harper soon after heard passionate cries and kissing. She got up and walked toward the shower cubicle and listened. The couple seems were now making love. Harper leaned on the glass walls of the shower cubicle trying to hear what was being said inside the shower room if any. The noise of the running water was swallowing up the couple's voice. Instantly a female voice screamed and Harper smiled and covered her mouth. As soon as the scream sound ended the door to the shower room was opened and Harper felt like someone pushed her aside as she ended up staggering backward. She heard footsteps leaving the shower room. She could see the water imprints of her feet and the water droplets from her body. The shower water stopped running, and the man started humming the song by Elinadeivid called I touched ladybird and I got lucky. After a while Harper heard a female voice talking.

"I am scared I am going to lose you. Darling let's start again and forget about all this."

The male voice stopped humming the song and replied.

"So, our son just die in vain?"

"I will give you another one."

"What if they take that one too?"

"We can go far away from here."

"That's not the point. They took our son. I will make them pay for that. They messed up with the wrong person."

"You might end up dead. You can't fight the whole country? Forget about all this."

"Too late now. They will come after me now?"

"Why. Let's run away."

"I shot her."

"Who?"

"The doctor who killed our son."

"So, all the blood you were covered in was hers?"

"Yes.

"But minutes ago, you said that she was not dead?"

"She is still alive."

"Start making sense. Is she dead or not? That was too much blood on your clothes to leave anyone alive."

"Hard to explain. We will talk about this when I come back. Right now, I have to go."

"Let's make love again. Let's try for another baby. I think another baby will ease the pain."

"I can't I have to go Darling. We will try when I get back. I promise. I love you."

Suddenly the voices stopped, and the gadget set off a beeping sound. Harper looked gob-smacked for a while not knowing what was going on. She pinched herself. This was really happening. She walked out of the shower room and into the bedroom. The gadget was flashing a constant blue light. She sat down on the bed before another beep went off. She picked up the gadget and pressed a button. Suddenly she heard the door to the bedroom opening. She looked terrified and looked around. She could hear that a woman entered the bedroom sobbing softly and sat on the bed next to her. She looked on the bed next to her and saw the pressure of someone sitting on the bed but there was no one. The women slept across the bed crying. Instantly Harper heard the back door suddenly opened, and she heard footsteps coming upstairs and suddenly the bedroom door opened again. The body imprints from the bed disappeared. The crying voices stopped. There was silence for a while before Harper heard few running footsteps and the sound of kissing and suddenly Harper fell on the floor as if someone had pushed her down. She started hearing the squeaky noises made by the bed before the man growled like an animal followed by the soft passionate cries of a female voice. Another loud sound from the female and then there was silence for a while. Harper could only hear the heavily breathing that gradually decreased with time. Minutes later she heard the voices again.

"I am very scared."

"Why Darling?"

The man breathed heavily first and Harper could hear the sound of the couple snogging.

"I love you."

"I love you Richard."

Harper looked shocked as she laid on the floor listening to the conversations. After a while the conversation continued.

"You seemed nervous today Richard."

There was a moment of silence before the man chillingly replied.

"I am going to kill the Vice President today."

The voices stopped playing. Harper stayed on the floor for a while only to be sent flying by the beeping sound from the gadget. She quickly got up and sat on the bed thinking.

CHAPTER FIFTEEN

Later that night a Land rover Evoque parked outside the newly build research lab in the city. The window of the SUV was opened and cigarette smoke came out of the window into the thin air. It seemed like it was a very beautiful night with a cool breeze and cloudless skies. Inside was Harper. She sat inside listening to rock music smoking. After a while she picked up the gadget from the dashboard and keyed in some information. A beeping sound went off, but the sound was swallowed by the sound of the rock music. After a while another beeping sound went off and Harper turned off the music and reversed backward until she heard another beeping sound. Instantly she stopped the car and looked at the gadget and the watch she was now wearing on her wrist hand.

"Correct geo-locational position. Press enter to confirm." Message appeared on the screen of the gadget. Harper looked anxious for a while before taking a long breath and pressed the Enter function.

Suddenly she heard voices. One was a female voice, and the other was a male voice. It seemed they were in the car as the voices Harper heard seemed to have been coming from a contained environment.

"I need a driver. Someone who is very hungry. Someone not afraid to start a war. Someone who will drive my plan."

There was silence for a while.

"For this plan to work there must be some major incident."

"What do you have in mind Mrs. Vice President?"

There was a moment of silence.

"Professor. I need a revolutionist. Someone we can turn into an animal and get rid of when our plan has taken effect. I am afraid we might not find someone like that,"

"Anyone can be a revolutionist. Anyone can be turned into an animal."

"Not everyone Professor. Some people are born like that. This is not something you can teach someone."

"Trust me, I have seen on television a toothless bird fighting a huge crocodile after her eggs were eaten by the crocodile."

Harper listened attentively as the voices were played. In the end, she heard the last voices.

"Here is the file of our potential subject. Get in touch and initial the project."

After that Harper heard the sound of the door opening and closing before she felt like being jerked as if the car had started moving. The voices stopped, and the gadget sent out a beeping sound. Later that evening Harper returned to the guest house and switched on the television and listened to the news.

The Vice President was on the news addressing the nation.

"Today is a sad day for our country. We shall stand together against terrorists and people who will threaten our way of life. They can terrorize our people but together we shall stand strong. Last week we mourned our President and I say to you all let's continue with the plan he laid for us. We shall give every citizen a serial number and everyone shall pay for this service, for protection throughout their life. We will do everything we can to make sure that you are safe. I know some will argue that this will infringe their privacy and their freedom but let me take this opportunity to tell you that the world is changing. We have new threats and therefore this project is not just essential but fundamental to our security and our future lives. The insurance companies shall cover everyone concerned."

Harper switched to the other channel. On the news was an anchorwoman report.

"This just in. Two planes had disappeared on the radar carrying passengers. The planes both sent distress signals at the same time before they were 'lost' as one of the tower staff put it. No one knows the probable cause of this but speculation is focused on the terrorists loyal to the murdered magic-word killer. Some say the planes both were carrying the government officials who both claimed to have been shot by the magic-word killer. No one knows exactly. Conspiracy theorists are arguing that the government is to blame for all this.

Harper switched to a different channel. There was news as well.

"A lot of people had gathered outside the hospitals threatening to sue the doctors there and calling for the closures of these hospitals after it came to light that a lot of women and children were selected to be tortured and experimented on before being killed. It seemed there was a gross misuse and negligence on the part of the hospital managers. People were campaigning for the dismissal of the managers concerned. The government had refused to comment but threatened to get all the demonstrators arrested which was received with scorn. Their argument is that it incited people to take the law into their own hands especially following the massacre of the doctor's in court months ago."

Harper looked on the gadget as it was flashing. At first, she ignored the gadget, but the gadget started flashing blue and orange lights quickly. She panicked. She looked at the gadget as she was undressing now just in her lingerie she walked toward the bed and picked up the gadget. There was a message on the gadget.

"Danger of death. Change geolocation coordinates now."

She read the message and stood speechless. Afraid and confused she panicked. Quickly she wore her t-shirt and about to put on her Elinadeivid jeans the door was forced open and a woman stood in front of her. She looked at her body and moved her eyes down to the Elinadeivid jeans that were in her ankles.

"Very nice."

When Harper looked down to cover herself a gunshot sound rocketed the guest house and the female intruder walked to the dying Harper and with her thump caressed her lips as she breathed her last breath. The intruder picked up the gadget and removed the watch from Harper's hand and entered the main house. Isabella and Andrew were lying on the carpet dead next to each other. An Elinadeivid song I touched ladybird and got lucky was playing in the background. The female intruder stopped at the door and looked at the dead couple before leaving.

In another city Scarlett, Harper's best friend was going out of a huge mansion when a delivery driver arrived in a van.

"Oh miss. Scarlet?"

"Yes."

"Please sign here."

Requested the delivery man handing a gadget to Scarlett to sign electronically her signature.

After signing Scarlett quickly opened the package. There were 30 small microchip memory cards, and a typed A4 document. It was titled; The Vice President: The Independent Adjudicator. She entered her car and started reading the document. She sat in the driver's seat her heart beating very fast. Soon after she drove off. In the hilly mountain road leading from her mansion on one of the bends a car had crashed and on the edge of the mountain. A man was lying in the road. Scarlett stopped the car and was about to go out and help when she took a quick glance at her passenger seat. The A4 document was out of the envelope. This was because of the harsh breaking the time she suddenly stopped. She looked around and quickly got back into the driver's seat before quickly reversing and running for her life.

CHAPTER SIXTEEN

Sometime in the past the day the Vice President opened the research lab.

The Professor and the Vice President were outside on the balcony having drinks and talking.

"I knew you are a woman of substance. This is the project that suits you. You have the world dancing for you. This does not come cheap and you must go out of your way but in the end, you will like the results. You can rule this world if you really want."

"Yes, I am listening."

Replied the Vice President.

"For years, I have tried to come up with a plan, a world map of everyone all at one point. Over the years, I have discovered that each one of us is different. Take twins for example, no matter how similar they are their DNA will be different. So, I came up with this plan. If we are all different. It will be easy to give each one a serial number. Over the years, I have been able to link everyone's DNA to a corresponding serial number."

"What are you saying Professor?"

"Let's put it this way. I am the puppet master. All my puppets are linked by serial numbers and I can make all either dance or carry objects through this serial number. Imagine when I cannot only use my hands to move the puppets but imagine when I can move them by word of mouth."

"Professor what you are saying is years away from now."

"OK let me entertain you even more. Imagine when I can control all these puppets through my thoughts through my mind?"

"That will be something. How would this work in the real world?"

"Over the years, I have worked on this technology. This is based on young kids growing up. The best way to communicate with them as they grow up is through phrases that are imprinted on their brain. In turn the brain saves these phrases and every time the baby hears these phrases it responds automatically."

"Yes, go on."

"Yes, Mr. Vice President the trick is in saying the correct word at the right time. Instead of using strings to make the puppets dance here we use coded phrases or words to achieve desired objectives. In this case, we just say words like dance, shake your booty, jump, kneel and the puppet will respond accordingly. In sophisticated scenarios, you the puppet master will only think about jumping and then the puppet will actually jump."

"Professor human minds are more complicated than puppets."

"So, I have given people serial numbers based on their DNA traits. So, I know who is who. Then I link serial numbers and programmed codes. So, if it's serial AB for example after implanting a chip all I need to do is to programme that person to be able to control the program itself but without him knowing it."

"How is that possible Professor?"

The Professor smiled and sipped his drink first. He looked away for a while first and then looked at the Vice President.

"Have you ever head of a game called word search?"

"You mean that puzzle everyone plays like a crossword?"

"Exactly?"

"Really how is that so?"

"We make the subject control the program and talk to the program but without knowing so. We let the subject say the words that will make the program achieve what we want."

"That must be something. Are there any laws regarding all this?"

"Mrs. Vice President what I am proposing is beyond human laws and all that stuff. It's either you want to rule the world or not? If you want, then you are the law you are the rules. Forget about privacy forget about laws and rights. You are the law. Are you with me?"

"Like I said Professor there is a lot of weight on my shoulders. I am answerable to the whole public."

"So, you are not ready then. In the end, they will accept this as the norm."

"How can that be achieved at such a scale?"

"I have been working on this for years now."

The Professor looked around to make sure that no one was looking or listening.

"The method works best with a chip. How you are going to implant it is not my problem, but I have seen hunters shot the chips inside the birds with pallet guns. The chips are very small."

"So that explains the $billions spent already because I was wondering where all that money was spent,"

"Exactly. It cost money. Just imagine collecting everyone and matching their DNA to a unique serial number and implanting these chips together with programming and maintain the infrastructure and the computer capabilities."

"OK Professor but my question is how are we going to achieve this?"

"That's when the doctors come in you will need some sharp shooters as well because not everyone will agree to this."

"So, I command everyone just with that?"

"Absolutely. The idea from here is to set up booby traps so that the subject say exactly what we want and once he or she has said that, then the program actually controls him and carries out our desired goal."

"So why not let others just say the words and achieve what we want?"

Queried the Vice President.

"Imagine a program where it accepts everything it hears. That subject is doomed. In that case, there are bigger chances that we will be caught because that subject will start to notice some strange behavior. Image when someone shouts shit, and the program starts moving that person's inside ready for disposal and then someone comes and say recycle. Then the excreted matter then starts being recycled mixed with fresh food. Definitely that subject will cry foul play."

"I see what you mean Professor so what is the solution for this."

"Have ever heard of voice picking a method used some years back?"

"I think I have read about it somewhere in one of the warehouse management books."

"Yes. That's the one. In this case only the voice of the picker is used to command the scanner and the whole picking process. Likewise, here we program the voice of the subject to be the only voice to command the system."

"That is well advanced."

"This is the future. Imagine you have stumbled on a plan to kidnap and murder you but you know this person is under your plan what do you do?"

"I guess send the special forces to shoot him down." Replied the Vice President.

"In your case, maybe but imagine when all you can do is hack his system and make sure that his system responds to everyone or your specialized assassins?"

"What are you saying Professor?"

"Imagine when you can send an army of voice commanders toward your enemy each saying a word that activates the next command to achieve your desired goal and choking your enemy to death."

"Professor these things cannot happen in real world only in dreams."

The Vice President looked at the Professor perplexed by the idea and just failing to believe that can happen contemplating the possibilities.

"This is now. I have the technology but do you have the guts to see this through?"

"What do I have to lose? What are we looking at here?"

"If this comes out we are looking at murder, modern day slavery, possession of weapons of mass destruction as this can kill millions just like that. We are looking at abuse of privacy rights, manipulation, abuse, violations of laws all of which carry a death sentence."

The Vice President looked very worried. The idea was very tempting, but the risks outweighed the benefits.

"The risks Professor if it comes out I am dead meat."

"For sure but stealth, precisions and ruthless is needed."

"What can I do with this what I can't do now?"

"Mrs. Vice President you were not listening to me. This is the Holy Grail of all Grails. Imagine killing someone in his sleep no matter where he or she is in the world just by saying a command. You can control everyone. The program works with anything that has a chip and have a serial number. You can program a plane to crash anywhere you want if the chip is installed and you can identify the serial number. No one else will have any power than you. You will rule the world. The question is. Do you have the guts to see this brilliant plan through?"

"I guess I need time to think about all this."

THE END

Elina Salajeva